Red Light

Red Light

Superheroes, Saints, and Sluts

edited by Anna Camilleri

ARSENAL PULP PRESS

VANCOUVER

ARSENAL PULP PRESS
Suite 200, 341 Water Street
Vancouver, B.C.
Canada V6B 1B8
arsenalpulp.com

The publisher gratefully acknowledges the support of the Canada Council for the Arts and the British Columbia Arts Council for its publishing program, and the Government of Canada through the Book Publishing Industry Development Program for its publishing activities.

Editing and selection by Anna Camilleri
Cover illustration and design by Suzy Malik
Text design by Shyla Seller
Linocut illustrations on pages 2, 8, 132 and 182 by Anna Camilleri

Printed and bound in Canada

Library and Archives Canada Cataloguing in Publication:

Red light : superheroes, saints and sluts / Anna Camilleri, editor.
ISBN 1-55152-184-9
1. Women in popular culture. 2. Women in mass media.
I. Camilleri, Anna
HQ1154.R428 2005 305.4 C2005-903774-1

ISBN-13 978-1-55152-184-8

Publication Notes

karen (miranda) augustine's "Beyond Dis/Credit: Divine Brown" was originally published in *Fireweed: A Feminist Quarterly*, no. 79, Winter 2003; reprinted by permission of the author.
An earlier version of Lori Hahnel's "Nothing Sacred" first appeared in *FreeFall Magazine*, Volume XIV, no. 1, Spring 2004; reprinted by permission of the author.
Collin Kelley's "Why I Want to Be Pam Grier" was originally published online in *Blaze: A Literary Magazine*.
Michelle Mach's "How to Become a Rodeo Queen" was previously published in *Mslexia*, Issue 19, Fall 2003; reprinted by permission of the author.
Barbara Jane Reyes's "the siren's story" was previously published in *Nocturnes Review*, Issue 3, 2004; reprinted by permission of the author.
Sara Elise Seinberg's "fuck you, i'm wonder woman" first appeared in *Will Work for Peace: New Politcal Poems* edited by Brett Axel (Trenton, NJ: Zeropanik Press, 2000).
Eva Tihanyi's "Barbie's Father Has a Nightmare," "At The Bar: Girls' Night Out," and "Janis Joplin Would Have Loved You" are reprinted from *Restoring the Wickedness* (Saskatoon, SK: Thistledown Press, 2000) by permission of the author.

Contents

Jezebel to Joplin: Female Icons Re-Imagined

An Introduction by Anna Camilleri

> Venus of what universe am I?
> I live in a glass house
> with glass bells
> and glass horses;
> how rarely do I stand face to face
> with my own forces.
>
> - Judy Grahn, *The Queen of Swords*

1. Topologies and Topography

I climbed into a car, intent on travelling west until I could taste salt—the Pacific Ocean, as far away from home as I could get without boarding a plane. I was in my early twenties, and hell-bent on going somewhere. It didn't matter that I didn't know where I was going, had no money, and was depending on the kindness of three well-intentioned but possibly dangerous strangers, who were just as fly-by-night as me. I was on the road. It was mid-September; green fields had receded like the tide. Amber, saffron, and crimson dominated the landscape.

I snapped photos through the front dash, many of them imprinted with my right index finger. Mostly, I looked out the window and jotted word-strings in my notebook: *Taut. Topographic. Tongue. Tongue on taut topography. Graphic to tongue taut top.* I was seduced by the possibilities; every jut of rock, every roll of hill reminded me of bodies I had tasted.

And then, I saw her. Shortly after crossing the Canadian-American border in Sarnia, she sped past in the left lane with hardly a sound. She was lean, long-legged, large-breasted, and covered in mud. This, my first sighting of the Mudflap Girl, happened in Michigan State, but I soon discovered that she is not bound by province, region, or geography. She is on every highway and freeway in North America, and perhaps around the world, protecting the underbelly of 18-wheel big rigs from dirt, sleet, and salt. My notepad simply says: *Woman on truck. Who is she? Why is she there?*

Since that day, I've encountered the Mudflap Girl — also known as the Silver Goddess of the Highway — through the windows of borrowed or rented vehicles in Jasper, British Columbia; Madison, Wisconsin; Redding, California; and many places in between. She captured my imagination, and I began to wonder: What would her story be, if she could tell it? Would she tell us about the marketer who dreamt her up, and all of the places she's been to? Would she tell us about "her" product line — the baby Ts, fridge magnets, bumper stickers, baseball caps, coffee mugs emblazoned with her image — and how she hasn't seen a dime from any of it? Would she tell us about Barbie, her not-so-distant relation, and what they're really up to when they're not on the open road? Would she tell us that we don't know the first, or the last, of it?

2. Dislocations and Magnetisms

Some say that icons are born, but it is public recognition — a devoted following, an audience, a "market" — that creates them. Born of our imaginations, desires, and fears, they are emblematic of our cultural climate on every front—social, political, spiritual, and economic. While some icons come in and out of focus, or fashion, they are here to stay.

The female as represented in western popular culture has been a timeless yet culturally unstable site—from the rise, fall, and re-emergence of the Goddess, to changing notions of the mother and social mores surrounding the slut. This instability, coupled with the tension between desire and repulsion, is precisely what produces the female icon. Construed and contested by men and women alike, the female icon is a site where our culture attempts to stabilize the female; to make her static, sterile, consumable.

Female icons reflect cultural sublimation of fear of the feminine in all of its manifestations, on a mass scale. Because the icon doesn't exist as "real" — rather, as a beyond-our-grasp screen upon which we project, undesirable aspects of femininity are denied, re-written, controlled, contained, and of course, sold, in palatable morsels. The Mudflap Girl is illustrative of this, but she's not alone. The Woman-in-the-Red-Dress is another female icon, also seemingly without voice and story. She turns up in music videos playing air-guitar, wearing pencil skirts and severely bound hair—she is the powerless dominatrix. Stripped of power, the icon allows us to dislocate aspects of femininity that are potentially frightening and place them in a repository while marking the boundaries of socially sanctioned, biologically determined femininity. When female icons are not only embraced, but engaged and re-imagined beyond those boundaries, there exists the potential to regain what is powerful, and powerfully experienced, about femininity—sexual agency, pleasure, and joy.

This book explores the threads of this fabric—the "underbelly" of female icons, and their significance in the lives and imaginations of women (and a few men). Here, female icons are re-imagined as "dangerous, as volatile matter, as blowing the whistle on the confines on femininity."[1] Greater than one-dimensional representations of "girl power," female icons elucidate the complexity in the lives of women, as well as cast a light — a red light — on the personal and public mythologies that create them.

Red Light encompasses icons stripped of sexuality and sexual agency, in addition to those who are highly sexualized — the Virgin Mary alongside Wonder Woman and Jezebel — each open to broad interpretation, each reflecting cultural dis-ease, and each riddled with troubling and important questions. In the smoke-and-mirrors terrain of female icons, the absences speak volumes. Those who are seldom taken up as icons in mass culture — women of colour, queer women, and women of diverse gender experience — are featured in *Red Light*, and how. Explorations of the "Indian Princess," the "Black Bitch," and the Bollywood seductress not only redress, but sear the lacquer right off of well-travelled colonial and racist epithets (see Boudreau, Moïse, and Singh). Those who are maligned and pathologized – witches, bitches, cougars, cunts, whores, and so-called crazy women – are celebrated here (see McKinley, Banerji, Bridgforth, and Cullis). The show stoppers – largely unknown despite mass exposure – shimmy into new narratives in which nocturnal emissions spill and refract in a house of mirrors (see Foad, Gottlieb, Hornick, Melusine, and Tihanyi). Icons that are steeped in a benign heteronormativity – domestic and do-gooder public servant "Goddesses" who are "naturally" selfless, demure, and morally upright – are redeemed by their portrayers (see Hahnel, Hammond, Simmers, and Steidle). And personal icons, who have lived solely in the imaginations of their creators (see Augustine, Linton, and Sami), make their stunning debuts.

3. Articulations and Long-Term Memory

As a child, I didn't dream about being Barbie or a cheerleader—not that there would be anything wrong with that beyond its anatomical impossibility, for me or any other average girl. But in my dreams, I wasn't average. I was Alpha Girl—a girl who could not be lost, because nothing can exist without a beginning, and Alpha Girl was there at the exact moment of articulation.

Besides her impeccable sense of timing, she also had the power to save other children from unthinkable horrors, held the Guinness World Record for the longest shot put, and was fiercely independent. The adventures of Alpha Girl were, of course, rife with conflict: just as she is about to swoop in to topple the neighbourhood Peeping Tom, she remembers that she doesn't know how to fly, and unceremoniously crashes to the ground. When pert breasts show up on the scene (her body), she squeals with delight, but soon after, notices that her place in the world now seems to be entirely mediated by the bumps that constantly assert their presence. Her delight becomes matched by ambivalence. Later, everyone (except for her equally marginalized friends and lovers) calls her a slut

— not in the appreciative, *You're so sexy!* way — and she eventually sets her own desires aside for a life in the doldrums that ticks out minutes and seconds like Betty Crocker's Easy-Bake. And you know what they say about watching a pot.

But Alpha Girl's problems weren't about utility. Her powers weren't faulty or compromised by proximity to copper, or nickel. No, Alpha Girl's dilemma, ironically, was one of memory. She routinely forgot who she was: a butt-kicking force of nature.

As a subterranean girl who didn't invest in Pippi Longstocking or even Nancy Drew, Alpha Girl was my very own superhero who embodied the qualities that I wanted and needed: strength, smarts, stubbornness, and a sense of "rightness" about my place on the planet. But even inside of the boundaries of my liminal childhood world where imagination ruled, Alpha Girl was subject to the rigours of social scrutiny that demanded she be a certain kind of girl, a girl that she wasn't—a one or the other kind of girl. Smart or strong. Moral or slutty. Competent or pretty.

Alpha Girl embodied my very-average-girl conflict: how can I be a butt-kicking force of nature in this world knowing full well that I shouldn't have to choose between one — smart, moral, competent — or the other — strong, slutty, pretty — and that none of those characteristics have anything to do with sex or gender, except for that which we insist upon?

When I set out across the country, I didn't know that I had left home in search of Alpha Girl—with her memory intact. I needed to find the Alpha Girl who knew her own strength and rightness and goodness, so that I could know my own. Its no small irony that a lost girl (me) set out in search of another lost girl (Alpha Girl) so that she (me) might find herself, only to discover another seemingly lost girl (the Mudflap Girl). In this landscape of lost girls, Alpha Girl swoops in and sashays with abandon, and yes, she also forgets some fundamental things about herself from time to time. I allow her this endearing quality because she is a superhero, carrying the hope of a very average, mortal girl.

Here then, are stories, poems, essays and works of visual art that make icons of lost girls, that gather together some of what has been misconstrued beyond recognition, as well as incendiary superheroes, saints, and sluts that defy any such categorizations. Harbingers one and all.

Anna

Anna Camilleri

[1] Brushwood Rose, Camilleri, "Introduction: A Brazen Posture." In *Brazen Femme: Queering Femininity* (Vancouver: Arsenal Pulp Press, 2002).

The New Beautiful

McKinley M. Hellenes

I. The Other Side of the Apple

History has always depicted us with fruit, or with fresh produce of some sort. The first time it happened, back in that goddamn garden, our big downfall was represented by an apple. What is so sultry and enticing about an apple, an everyday, kitchen-table sort of affair, I'll never know — though folks seem right spellbound with the idea. In another, it was lettuce — a whole garden of it going to waste behind a tall stone wall. Pregnant women were literally hiking up their skirts to scale the enclosure every five minutes, the silly cows — it really got on a body's nerves. So finally I told this one woman, "Give me your firstborn daughter, and I'll fork over the lettuce." I thought that'd fix her up right smart — I never thought the dumb bitch would actually agree to it! So there I was, saddled with this goddamn kid, and nowhere to put her but the tower. Stupid brat grew her hair so long she could have hung herself with it, and maybe she should have, considering what happened to that prince who was dumb enough to fall in love with her. I stopped growing vegetables after that, thought it might foil the common folk — superstitious as hell, those people — but they always seemed to find me. There was this one silly little girl who let herself get too pretty for her stepmother, the queen. She was supposed to be murdered, but only pretended to die, and instead was forced to make her way into the forest I enchanted specifically to keep her out of my hair when she was born, the little monster, but that never stops them for long. Before I knew it, she was living with those goddamn singing dwarves, who sang twice as loud when she started doing the washing up, though I never knew any man to so much as bat an eye when any other woman set about the household chores, the louts. So I figured I'd make a house call on our pretty little homemaker, a basket of fruit under my arm and a kindly look on my wrinkled old face — only this time, it really was an apple I offered her — I didn't want the kid getting all suspicious on me. Told her I'd eat the green part, and she could have the red part — I grew those apples myself so I knew which end I'd poisoned, and pretty little girls always want the red, rosy parts, miserable brats. And as for that forbidden fruit business, do you really think I'd have been so goddamn stupid as to accept a lowly apple? No sirree, I knew what I was about — and I'll never tell, never reveal what sort of tropical delicacy made me give up paradise for this place — but just you try setting foot into my garden and you'll discover the other side of the apple right enough, Missy. And I don't mean the sour green part. If I know you, you'll leave that to me, no questions asked. It's what I've always counted on.

II. Slipknot

In my family, when a woman turns thirty, she cuts her hair. Up until then, each one of us has the most astonishing head of hair, not one of which is like another. I remember thinking that I must be in the company of witches, for no ordinary women could grow such hair from an ordinary set of scalps: Aunt Emily's hair was long and thick and straight, that near-black colour that's common in us Scots-Aboriginal mixed bags. Aunt Melissa's was just as long and thick, but not nearly as silky, preferring instead to remain kind of puffy and soft and the colour of taffy. My mother's hair was so thick and wavy that it tended to go in every direction at once. Meanwhile, my own hair grows and grows towards the inevitable date of its undoing. Every day as I brush out my hair, feeling the weight of it in my hands, I can't help but think of the day when it must be sacrificed to the blade of the kitchen scissors. I even imagine myself in the backyard, dressed in some sort of black shroud, burning my hair upon its little funeral pyre, just as they did to women like us in the Dark Ages. Once, I asked my Aunt Emily why it is that the women in our family perform such a strange and morbid ritual. It was with a grim mouth that she explained to me, as though it was obvious, that when a woman turns thirty, she is simply too old for the vanity and bother of long hair — "And so off it goes," she said, as though she were really saying, "Off with her head!" I would later think of this as I read of how those condemned for witchcraft would be forced to cut their long hair to make sure they would not use their braids to hang themselves before they could be decently burned. I had no idea what a latent weapon I carried around with me at the nape of my neck – as potent as a cyanide tooth. It lent new meaning to the expression "Give them enough rope to hang themselves," for that was indeed what we, and perhaps all women like us through the ages, had been given. It made me wonder if my aunts were surreptitiously relieving themselves of the possibility of such an escape, preferring instead to burn at the stake if need be – and if you knew my aunts, you would know that would be just like them. And though I will miss my wild hair, I think perhaps they are wise – and that I, too, must embrace both blade and flame as my fate. Though I be a woman, and a heretic at that, let the bastards come to me. Let them engrave that on my skull.

III. Lament for the Cougar Lady

We knew they weren't witches, but it sounded better in the dark than crazy old hermits, so we said it anyway, and we said it often. I remember seeing them when I was just a kid, going through the paperback novels at St. Mary's Thrift Store on Cowrie Street. At first, I didn't know there was more than one of them – it was years before I figured that out – and I suppose it was Bergie I really noticed. She was the more leathery of the two, taller, stocky like a pit-bull, and broader than any woman I had ever seen. She had more of an attitude, if you want to know the truth, and I liked that. I liked the fact that you could wake up early on any given Saturday and meet Crazy head on, just by strolling down Main Street, Sechelt, British Columbia. I didn't know she had a name at the time, any more than I knew she had a sister who looked just like her. We just called her the Cougar Lady. I always wanted to talk to her, but it was implied that one didn't just go up and say "howdy-do" to a woman who trapped wild animals for exercise before breakfast – which we assumed consisted of some mangled and half-cooked body part of the morning's prey. So no one talked to her much. We chose instead to view her from behind lampposts, or skulking behind the war memorial across from the pet food store. As I got older, I inevitably got bolder, and I would stalk her through town, watching her fondle overripe produce at the local Save-On-Foods like all the lovers we assumed she had never had. She wore the same battered cowboy hat smashed down on her head, the same polyester blouse and old suede vest, year in and year out. She was probably born in that hat. She was as wind-brazen as Sinbad, as leathery as a forgotten apple core. My throat hurt whenever I looked at her, and though I would rather have died than admit it, I often laid awake at night, conjuring stories of the old woman who lived alone in the backwoods, bowie knife at her side. Sometimes I even imagined her stripping off that threadbare blouse, those old boots. In my mind I spun her in circles beneath the moon, threw her hat to the sky.

Nowadays, when children lurk furtively behind me in the grocery store line, I say her name ever so softly to myself as I clasp an avocado like a lover to my polyester heart.

Nowadays, I admit to everything.

IV. Wicked Witch of the East End

It was the bike I wanted, you understand. Forget broomsticks, or magic carpets, or astral hoo-ha — that flying bicycle was all I ever wanted in this world. Something I could traverse hurricanes in. And that little basket attached to the handlebars was my first introduction to the thrall of fetish. At night I dreamed of wicker twisting itself into demented shapes around my wrists and ankles, my hair weaving hampers in itself above me in my sleep. I was even willing to risk the pea green complexion just to lay my hands on that fabulous contraption for one split second of my insignificant little life. What a mount I would have between my quivering thighs, all glimmering rims and shiny chrome fenders, a real vintage crotch rocket. Before I saw that bike, I had no idea I even *had* a crotch — not in that tingly way. But imagining how that narrow leather seat would snuggle into my pubis changed me in ways I could not ignore. And I have to admit, I would be lying if I say I didn't have a thing for the shoes too — the ruby red slippers, those alluring preternatural pumps. I could see myself in a pair of those babies. What a stunner I would be, gliding over rooftops in my stiletto . . . and then I thought – high heels? Wouldn't sneakers be more appropriate for a punk kid like me? I mean, flying bike or no flying bike, let's be practical here. No wonder the old crone got caught under that house – she probably hooked her heel on the chimney and took a tumble. Well, no one was going to see me in my green-striped unmentionables, let me tell you – it was red-sequined Rocket Dogs all the way, or nothing. I would outsmart that little pigtailed bitch before she could squeal "Aunty Em!" Let's see who's in Kansas now, Dorothy – and it sure as hell isn't gonna be you, unless it's six feet under. I mean, who the hell did that little brat think she was, anyway, parking her bungalow on a witch's you-know-whats – not to mention interfering with a woman's love for her hog? Well, I for one wouldn't have it – and fuck that Glinda too. What a superior bitch. The only reason you don't see her riding around on a broomstick like everyone else is cuz she's got it lodged so far up her ass she can barely see straight. The woman can no longer bend at the waist! She's no match for me. Just let her try to catch me. Me and my flying bike would make quite a silhouette descending from the sky, right towards little Dorothy's bedroom window with only my vermillion heels to light my way.

V. Bergie Speaks

If they knew my name they'd call me Bergie an' I been told I was born here, or here abouts – though I don't rightly remember, only that I was suddenly here and breathin' God's good air and then just as sudden there was my sister Minnie trundlin' around, hangin' on the back a my shirt-tail. I don't recall much of the time before Minnie's gettin' born, just that I had a mama and after that I ain't got much a nobody, though our Old Dad was always around somewheres, choppin' wood or somethin', bein' strong an useful and quiet like men were in those days, though there ain't been no men around here for longer'n I can recall as I don't much hold with 'em myself and Minnie don't hold much with nobody but herself an' me a course but then she ain't much got a choice in the matter. There ain't much different 'bout things out here since I was a wee thing, though things have changed considerable over in that town we go to sometimes for sellin' my cougar skins an' that's how we got to be called what they call us, though Minnie never was no use at trappin' and killin' animals. She don't come into town much anyways, though I think most folks don't notice when there's two of us in any case, so it's more a case a me bein' called what I am an' not the both of us anyhow. Minnie's the quieter one a us girls, more like our ol' dad than I am in that regard, an' our mama never lived long enough to contribute much a anythin' when it comes to that. Though I dunno what good it does a body to be quiet, loud, or otherwise when don't nobody talk to us to our faces in that town when we goes there, and when we goes there together everbody figures they's seein' double, though at any other time they don't think a us for any reason at all, so I don't think they bother keepin' count anyhow. They forgets us soon's we go, and then they play at bein' shocked next time they sees us standin' side by side. I expect that's why Minnie don't come into town much anymore, she just grunts somethin'r another and thumps off to the bedroom in that way she has a doin' things when she's set on doin' somethin other'n what you want her to. That might be on account a what else folks been callin' us, but I told them people I never ate a child in my life, 'cept maybe a bear cub when there ain't nothin' else, but you don't see them bears runnin' round makin' up stories about broomsticks an' what have you. Besides, Minnie's the one takes care a the kitchen round here anyhow, though folks ain't seen her around much anymore. Maybe they figure I run outta kids.

VI. Memoirs of the Schoolyard Bwitch

It was a typical playground taunt. Only no one was actually brave enough to enunciate the obscenity — so we changed it ever so slightly to accommodate the sensitive ears of our playground referees, the dreaded teacher's aides. We called each other "Witch-with-a-capital-B." Delphine was a W.W.C.B. because she was a bully. Maria was one because she was Delphine's cousin. Jessa was one because she was prettier than the rest of us, and I was one because I was smarter than Jessa. It was, in a way, the only system by which kids with different status could be seen as equal. If we displeased someone, and it could be anyone, even the lowliest among us – we could be labelled with the dreaded B-word . . . or maybe the W-word. It was never clear to us what exactly we were being called, and I suppose most of the time, it was really a double whammy, because either way, we were something we didn't want to be known as. If we were bitches, we were mean, and if we were witches, it was only because we lacked the guts to be bitches – so although no one wanted to be either, we all secretly preferred the B-word. I always thought it was strange that we saw the word bitch as being more powerful, and therefore more desirable, than the word witch. Witches were meaner, sneakier than anyone else – they were crafty, evil, altogether the most ominous symbols known to first-graders. And yet we preferred to be known as female dogs rather than to tap into that power. Our dads called our moms bitches when they wanted to reduce them, diminish their power – I could see no reason to want to inherit the legacy. As far as I saw it, a witch wouldn't put up with that kind of crap. A witch would just put a hex on anyone who pissed her off, and that would be the end of it. Witches enchanted common household objects for their diabolical purposes. Witches commanded weather patterns. Witches wore black all day long, and black was tough to pull off. The best part of being a witch would be that no one would know what you were going to do next, because you could do anything you wanted. Think of the opportunities when others call you a witch, with or without the B. Consider yourself empowered, my pretty. Take that broomstick out for a test drive. Whack all the dirty old bastards you pass upside the head with the bristles on your slick new ride. Throw back your head and cackle, girl, and don't bother plucking those "unsightly hairs" from your wart. Haven't you heard? Ugly is in this year. Ugly is the new beautiful.

fuck you, i'm wonder woman

Sara Elise Seinberg

i have cinched my waist
to distort
and accentuate
these wide and mighty rolling hips
the childbearing hips you love.
i have worked my thighs into granite for you
because you like them wrapped tight and warm
around your neck,
my feet entangled in your
long
red
cape.
i have learned to accessorize wisely.
my stylish hipster ensemble is
stunningly draped in defense.
while my elegant forearm bracelets
provide a jaunty complement
to my soft and milky skin,
they also repel your attacks.
fashion armor vogue for today's woman.
i have a magic lasso
because i have to fucking tie you up
to force your honesty.
i need a rope from another planet
to pry the truth
from your pursed and smirking lips.
i have knee-high, harder, faster, fuck-me red boots.
my boots have a voice
that essentially says,

"excuse me,
sir,
would you mind
politely
backing the fuck up."
my boots are tasteful
and my boots are strong.

so when you come home from lois' at three a.m. high on smack, as plunder has become boring, conquer so sublime, sobriety so eighties . . . and you quietly snake the keys to my jet from my utility belt as i sleep naked and alone awaiting your form on the mattress next to me, and you take my jet without asking, the only one of its kind, and on the nod, too fucked up to even fly your own tired ass, and you crash my shit into an untouched tribe, then talk a ganga shit 'bout saving them from their primitive ways, never acknowledging that a heroin mishap dropped you in their midst, and then you begin to colonize them, control them, in the name of progress, and then have the audacity to *tax* them for that privilege.

i don't think i'm overreacting
"due to pms"
as you so often chide me
to be so bold as to say to you

fuck your speeding bullets
fuck your tall buildings
fuck your single bound

superman,
fuck you

i'm
wonder woman.

Grandma the Indian Princess and Other Settler Fairy Tales

Michelle Boudreau

I know — you're picturing the prototypical Pocahontas: barefoot in short-short leather fringe, a few beads, and some feathers to accessorize. As for makeup, just a few random stripes of colour on her face and she's ready to go. Low maintenance for a Princess. She doesn't even need to be from any particular tribe, you can throw the meanings of different Nations' symbols right out, or stick them all in a bag and shake it really good. Instant Indian Grandma, ready to be taken out at your convenience — on genealogy websites, when talking to any given Native person, even at parties. It was a fad for the Virginian colonists; why not bring it back?

Yeah, she's been around a long time, the Indian Princess. Well, first she was an Indian Queen, but she was demoted. Her image in drawings from the British colonies is widespread — though how she managed to look so good after escaping all those massacres and blanket-induced smallpox epidemics is a well-kept beauty secret. Supine amidst random "New World" exotica, she is virginal, proud, fertile, and incredibly desirable — not unlike the "New World" itself. That's what they say, but I know better.

Grandma has been keeping several secrets. We knew her back in the day; her untamed wilderness was well-known territory to us. You might not have heard about the millions she's enjoyed, the towns and villages, and her waterways and ports were well-used, I tell you. Complicated and diverse democratic political systems existed to ensure that she was evenly shared. I wonder if Grandpa knew what she was up to before he stuck his flagpole in her beautiful brown earth.

Another secret is her sister — dirty, easy, and probably drunk, the Squaw gets what she deserves. Whereas Indian Princesses only seem to exist in the past, the Squaw is everywhere and anytime. What can be done to a

Squaw without reprisal is so limitless that if dozens of us end up buried in a pig farm, few notice or care. An Indian Princess would never get drunk, get horny, or become a sex worker, so she must be safe – except in cases of mistaken identity. Shadowed by the Princess, the Squaw hides secrets of her own. She was not so derided once. In fact, her name probably originated from an Algonquian word for "woman," which was used with great respect in related terms such as that for the Clan Mother – until colonizers misappropriated the term. Thus a term used for generations to describe our mothers, sisters, and daughters, came to reflect the legitimization of the colonial patriarchy's most horrific violence against us.

The Indian Princess's claim to royalty is also specious. The problem being that, as many Native writers have explained, the concept of "royalty" didn't exist among First Peoples. No Kingdoms, no Kings, no Princes – although it's much less popular to allege having male Indian ancestors. Vine Deloria Jr. says that if all the claims of Indian Princess ancestors were actually true, there would have been no male children for generations; just thousands of Princesses, marrying white men in droves. Of course, out of the great number of those claiming a relation to "American Indian Royalty," it's probable that many actually do have Native female ancestors. Some of them might even have been daughters of important Native men, such that the word "Princess" was just a misnomer. If so, that's great. I can empathize, myself having canoed the rivers of being a light-skinned person recently discovering one's Native identity. The more the merrier, as far as I'm concerned. We cannot allow the scarcity imposed by colonization to dictate the boundaries of our national identities.

No, it's not real Indian Grandmas, but the mythical Indian Grandma – or great-Grandma, or great-great-Grandma – the Indian Princess who is alive and well in the North American popular imagination that I have a problem with. You have to wonder what's so reassuring about her that her image is held so dear. The role she plays over and over – rescuing/rescued by the white man, eager to accept colonization, destined to disappear into history – is fundamental to the settler psyche. She not only is from America, but she *is* America, so much so that her image is its archetypal visual representation. The message that Disney's Pocahontas and

Tiger Lily whisper is so soothing to the consciousness of settlers that they feel the need to introduce her to their children to this day: "We needed each other. This was a love affair. I wanted you to take me, I longed to be consumed by you so much that the very earth and wind of my body compelled me toward my destiny." Her being conquered was not a violent rape, not genocide of unimaginable proportions, but a fairy tale, a romance novel. The attempt to appropriate her as a figment of one's own past may well be a means of assuaging any potential guilt, and is in fact actively used to eschew responsibility. When faced with a real live unhistorical Native person, this fictional Grandma is knee-jerk defensiveness.

I wish by no means to suggest that Native women who married white men were as they are represented by this myth. My own ancestors are among these, and I don't see them as sell-outs, abandoning of their people, or any such thing. From the comfortable vantage point of hindsight, it is easy to presume that these women should have somehow known what was to happen. It may be convenient to think in terms of what we know now, that the European colonists they were meeting and exchanging with had a fundamentally different agenda from the other nations they interacted with, traded with, and intermarried with as a customary part of international relations, to pretend that these women did not come from nations in which political strategies were actively discussed among women as part of their community responsibilities, in which these women made sound and intelligent political decisions involving how to relate to other nations whether friendly or hostile.

Pocahontas herself may have had a very good reason for protecting Captain John Smith, but that reason is lost to history. It is clear from Smith's diaries that they were not romantically involved, and indeed, the real Pocahontas married another man and accompanied him to the land of his birth. She never returned home, but died of smallpox in England as did so many of her people back across the ocean. In the messy world of reality, colonization does not end with a fantasy wedding, or even an orchestrally climactic kiss.

Many of us with mixed Native heritage, including my own Métis family, managed to assimilate or "pass" into white culture. The few of us who survived had to do this in some way. This was not our destiny, but a temporary strategy employed by some. In spite of the role of inter-marriage in the plan for our genocide, our identity as First Peoples does not get washed away by mixture with "white blood." We are, as the poet Chrystos says, "Not Vanishing." Many of us who have hidden or neglected our Indigenous selves are trying to find our way back to the path of all our relations. In this awkward process it is inevitable that at some point we must face our own internalized racism, unravelling the Indian Princess and the Squaw in order to find an integral and genuine identity.

Sugar Zero

Rima Banerji

For Aileen Wuornos, executed by the state of Florida on October 9, 2002

The American miracle: that of the obscene . . .

> Snapshots aren't enough. We'd need the whole film of the trip in real time; we'd have to replay it all from end to end in a darkened room, rediscover the magic of freeways and the distance . . . and the speed and live it all again on the video at home in real life.
>
> — Jean Baudrillard, *America*

> . . . your tenderest skin
> strung on its bow and tightened
> against the pain. I slipped out like an arrow.
>
> — Olga Broumas, *Beginning With O*

I dreamt of endless freeways. I dreamt of hustlers and travelling,
some way out of here, my first home, a starved and marginal place,
each young bone of its frame waiting to break its fast of hunger.
the streets of my small town only lead to dead ends: make a road for me.

You just laughed. You taught me how to cross the street, look both ways, holding me back from the dangers I loved. You shouted out all the female mantras of safety:

Be careful when you walk home Don't walk alone in a dark alley Don't walk alone at all Don't drive by yourself at night Check your car, lock your doors, roll up the window, look in the backseat (someone might be hiding in there) Don't smoke Don't drink Don't do drugs Just say no Don't answer the door Don't pick up the phone Don't talk to strangers Don't have sex with strangers Just don't have sex, at least until you're married Don't marry a bad boy Don't date one either Don't look him in the eye Don't let anybody in Don't let him in Don't let her in You don't want to be a freak do you Crazy fucking bitch Don't let them think you're a slut Don't let them think you're a lesbian Don't let them think you're a dyke a fucking whore a fucking dyke Don't be crazy Don't be political Don't talk back to me Don't wear anything skimpy You know what I mean Just don't wear anything that might get you raped You don't want to be raped do you Just don't Nice girls don't, so just

DON'T

These commandments didn't work. I wore them like handcuffs on the falsely accused. Sex was the key that unlocked them, sex my rebel money and music, sex the bow that sent the arrow of my body spinning in the air.

And before lust, you gave me a mimic to play with: the dull-faced girl lassoed into marriage, as if Wife and Mother were the only brands worth wearing, placated by trademarks mundane or bovine. Never wanted to be saddled with suburban husbands or stubborn babies. Or become a woman, solitaire, chaste, unregenerate – loneliness is no prize to me, nothing alone lives; it just lasts. Never surrendered to the joyless luck of being alone with myself: that's what sleep and death are for.

You tell me that union is the true meaning, the true purpose of a woman, and her end. But I hated the end, only saw the beginning of things, the unfolding, unanchored, planned liberty of being, no real direction or destination, just the mouth of something new to spit out, a dark sojourner tumbling to her truth. I found my escape route early, hitch-hiking on the back of a truck with any outsider who would take me for a ride.

I could have been anyone and I was, dark nimbus cloud of a girl, roaming with the wheels, whirling towards the next stop, another new place on the map named Death Valley or Lynchburg.

And you look at me with eyes soured like dead love. You cluck at me, common pigeon, stupid gull. My ways are too free. I'm an easy woman. Women shouldn't be easy, you tell me, they should be tough, hard puzzles, maze of gutted labyrinth with no way out. Easy is just too comfortable, too simple. And I am one of those slack and languid women, and I like it. Don't want to be too difficult: a woman can die from complications. You know what you are too: a hard woman, bought with an even harder diamond. Not me. I *am* easy, disposable, a convenience like anything else you rent or buy, eventually throw out. The men like girls like me, I have no face to condemn them, just the flowing shape of a woman, my cunt young and loose, a one-size-fits-all garment for their slow bodies, their sagging lives.

I want to say: you shouldn't be afraid. I may be easy, but it's hard for any man to own me. I memorized all your rules, but I'm no longer under arrest. I took off the handcuffs, I'm the arrow, remember? I haven't stopped spinning in the air, I get by, just carry myself like a boning knife, just shoot the johns who tell me I'm the colour of mud, that I smell like it too, all that soft slough and sleaze, but they're just smelling themselves, because I may look like mud, but they're dead and buried in it. Yes, I am one of those women, dirty and slack, but sister, I still move fast, fuck hard, speed murder liberty the drugs I wagered my life on. You were the one who taught me bastard love, or how to kill: I watched you slaughter chickens, crimson poisoning the once-rich soil.

I'm tired now. I've come back to tell you: I've seen what you never will. I've seen myself untouched by fear, unbending, choking out the rules you made up to protect me. I've learned terror in my time. I have seen this country and its men, stretched out and bloody, and I will never regret it. *It was easy. I just got caught.* Now, not me alone, we are both falling, planted in mud – you, husbanding your animals and flowers, and I, watching the crimson flow.

And I know, I could have been anyone and I wasn't. I told my life what I wanted, but life is uncouth. It never asks me what I want. I tell it, but life won't listen, in fact it pretends not to hear, and does what it wants anyway, dragging me along, back to your handcuffs. So the arrow finally landed. I've stopped spinning. I don't regret it. Let me say this: I'll always be the snake to your sublime. So keep my mementos –

a sonata for the badlands, and a lyric for your dahlia face.

Mary Was . . .

Linda Dawn Hammond

and WHO in the HELL is Joseph
and does he support You and the babe
In the end they'd have turned her away
For squatting a stable
and dressing Jesus in rags
and HOW do You track down GOD for child support?
(Jesus, what a story!)
If Mary lived in Toronto
She'd be labelled (and it wouldn't be VIRGIN)

Artist's Statement

This is the story of the Virgin Mary, if she had attempted to apply for welfare as a single mother in Toronto. Based upon a true incident (involving a different Mary).

The series was created as an installation for the "Sex Show," which was temporarily housed in the former welfare offices on King Street in Toronto. It transformed the mailbox in which welfare recipients regularly deposited their monthly statements, located adjacent to a long corridor of interrogation rooms. Mary visited one such room.

The story is written upon such envelopes as the monthly cheques arrive.

In the photos, Mary is depicted giving birth to and then breastfeeding the glass baby Jesus. The former image is absent from most, if not all, artistic renditions of the Virgin, though one would assume that in spite of the parthenogenic nature of the conception, the birth was a somewhat more worldly act. In spite of the "hands on" nature of Jesus' bodily fluids, the Virgin's remain taboo.

— *Linda Dawn Hammond*

At the Bar: Girls' Night Out

Eve Tihanyi

Eve admits she's still
brooding over Adam, living
with her legs open, eyes closed,
mistaking blind sex
for blind faith

Persephone says she's finally
in love with Hades,
but he's no longer interested

Lilith downs a shot of tequila,
stays silent

Eve complains
she's bored with Adam, needs
more humour in her life,
more conversation

Persephone, near tears,
worries that *Hades* is bored with *her*,
doesn't know what to do about it

Lilith says this is why
she likes to fuck strangers

Janice Joplin Would Have Loved You

Eve Tihanyi

Between your thighs:
horses, motorcycles, men

Behind you:
the hearts you've won and tossed,
their metronome devotion
still ticking

You abhor such smooth monotony,
demand a music fast and improvised,
tempting and savage

You're tall and unpredictable;
no one's going to talk you down

My Sister Caddy

Rose Cullis

When my sister Caddy was born, she was already a diesel femme. She had a little blonde curl on the top of her head that the nurses loved to twist around their fingers and coo over.

That's what my mother said, anyway. Caddy was born three years before I was, and by the time I arrived, the single curl had spread into a headful of loose tousled ones, together with blue eyes and a smile so calculated in a toddler, it was terrifying. At three years old, my sister Caddy had already embarked on a career as a model girl. In the few photos from this period that my parents bothered to take or save, I'm bald and puling, but Caddy gazes directly into the camera – radiant and dimpled and only vaguely interested in what she holds in her arms: me.

There's a shadow in the picture, though – a shadow of my parents, posing for their own portrait, before Caddy was born, before they were married. My mother stands in a bikini, one leg carefully placed before the other, like a beauty queen cheerfully awaiting the judges' decision. My father stands beside my mother, scowling and uncomfortable – a skinny nerd in black-rimmed glasses, with thinning dark curls and acne scars. My mother doesn't realize that my father is wracked with rage. She thinks he's sweet and shy. She plans to feed him homemade butterscotch pies every night to fatten him up, but my father will turn out to be harder to please than that. He'll eat the pies, though.

Caddy was the first one to fight back. There was a lot to resist – especially for a radical femme in training. My parents had unusual taste in fashion. We were forced to sport pixie cuts and black oxfords until we were twelve. The result, needless to say, was a kind of social isolation. Caddy looked hideous in a pixie cut, and her nose grew long and pointed. My younger sister Charlie and I were increasingly shunned by Caddy, as pathetic projections of her own lonely and enforced ugliness. In response, I took a pencil to her school picture once, and coloured the tip of her nose in, for emphasis.

Caddy fought back with the same tools my father used. Her drama queen emerged, miraculously, as fully developed as his — like a god leaping from the head of Zeus. Caddy knew how to roll her eyes and twist her features into hideous expressions. She knew how to pitch forward in a seizure, spastic with ecstatic rage; how to make a psychotic break strike terror in the hearts of onlookers.

Caddy was my mad woman in the attic, going to the very end of the chain and laughing hysterically. She was my Catherine in *Wuthering Heights* — throwing open a window in the middle of a storm, so that she could get sick and die and get everyone back. But most of all — Caddy was *sex* for me. Sex and pornography and men and boys and tits and asses and naked women posing in the snow. Grinning at the photographer, nipples as hard as crystals.

One year, Caddy was still playing big dolls. The next year, she was dragging boys home and taking them upstairs to shower with her, or downstairs to the basement. I'd listen at the heating vents. Caddy would be whining and whimpering. "We're bad," she'd be saying. "Aren't we bad?"

I didn't want to think about what might happen if my father arrived home when one of the boys was upstairs in the shower with her. She wasn't even supposed to be holding hands yet.

Caddy started climbing into my bed at night, making a tent with the sheets so we could talk. I could tell what was going on. She felt guilty, and she needed to get me involved. She needed me — for the first time in my life — and I thrilled to her attention, even though the ecstatic look in her eyes made me feel uneasy. There was a girl in her class, she said, who sat at the back of the school bus, and let all the boys come and feel her up when the teachers weren't watching.

Who was that girl? I didn't know, but I did know that sex was something women did for men. Even though it confused me and felt difficult to integrate, I was an ascetic at heart, and I loved the idea of abandoning comfort and suffering for my sexuality. The first time I stuck a tampon in, I got it wrong. It pinched. I didn't know. I thought it was right. I thought that was what being a woman was all about. I went out with my family to Howard Johnson's for dinner that hot summer night with the tampon probably lodged horizontally in my cunt, blushing and turning down my eyes shyly when men looked at me.

Caddy noticed a shift in my attitude, and began teaching me in earnest – adding a pre-adolescent Charlie to the class, for good measure. She'd bring a boyfriend home, and arrange for our lessons. The boy would lie on the couch, and Caddy would direct us in the fine art of sex.

Charlie and I didn't mind, particularly. Caddy had never played with us before, and the games were relatively non-invasive. Under Caddy's direction, Charlie and I sucked, licked, and kissed key erotic zones, making sure we unzipped cramped penises and gave them enough room to expand comfortably. I was charmed by the tripartite structure of the male anatomy. Even though our father's penis loomed large in the economy of relationships in our family, I had never, luckily, seen it. I thought that boys just had one vaulting, velvet-headed member. When Caddy uncovered the wire-haired and wrinkled purses that came with, I felt like I was initiated into some esoteric and magical cult. Charlie and I found the glazed eyes of the boys rewarding, and we both felt really powerful. Caddy loved the performances.

I was always watching Caddy. Once, she showed me the points where perfect legs are supposed to come together. The upper thigh. The knees. The ankle bones. Caddy was perfect. She fashioned a kind of makeup table in her room, and sat at it – rubbing cream into her face, and then rubbing it off. She wore powder-blue eye-shadow and frosted lipstick. As her hair grew, her nose seemed to soften.

For a while, Caddy had a tough and occasionally vicious boyfriend named Keith. She was always attracted to the hard-core working class boys — as a kind of antidote to my father's fastidious brutality. She liked to bring me along when she went out with Keith in particular. I'd sit beside them in Keith's truck, looking nonchalant when Caddy unzipped his pants in heavy traffic.

Keith worked on a farm, and one day, Caddy asked me if I'd like to go with her on the bus to visit him. I was thrilled, and Caddy promised to show me new puppies to further seal the deal.

We waited at the bus stop early the next morning. It was late spring, and we both wore cotton print dresses that fluttered around us in the light sweet wind. Happy and hopeful. When we got to the farm, it wasn't the way I imagined it. It was set in dark scruffy woods, and the road in was muddy. The house looked like an early fifties suburban model home. The rooms inside were dark with cheap wood paneling, and the puppies had a raw smell. Keith was in a foul mood, and Caddy immediately went upstairs with him to try to make him feel better. I sat with the whimpering puppies and picked up a book. It was clearly trashy, so I immediately started searching for the dirty parts.

I looked up. Caddy was there. "Keith wants you," she said, and I dutifully went upstairs to see just what Keith wanted. He was lying naked in bed. Nothing new there. He slipped his hands down the back of my pants, and suddenly I lost interest in being obedient. I got up and walked to the window. The poplars outside looked damp and yellow. I couldn't see the sky. "Good girl," Keith said. "Save yourself till you're eighteen, and then I'll break you in."

Too late, I thought, which wasn't exactly true, but my sense of irony was like a crack of light.

It wasn't Keith I wanted. It was Caddy. Caddy. Caddy. Sometimes she'd come into our beds in the morning when Charlie and I were all sleepy, and feel the imprints from bedding or clothing on our skin. Her manicured fingers were as light as fluttering eyelashes. Years later, when I finally fell madly and incurably in love with a woman, I realized that she was some kind of strange cross between Caddy and my father. My lover had black-rimmed glasses and short curly hair, and she dressed like a man from the fifties — like my father in the photo. Sometimes — more often as time went by, and I couldn't get it right, whatever *it* was — she'd scream and bang her head and claw at her eyes in an agony of rage and disappointment. I recognized all this. Had been there before, felt uniquely capable of hanging in, and loving after. When we made love, and she sighed in my ear, "Don't stop, don't stop" — it was Caddy whimpering in the basement. Caddy giggling in the truck. Caddy with a difference. "What's the difference?" I cried to my lover once. "Why is being with a woman so beautiful?"

"Because," she said, "this time it's about *your* pleasure."

Gas stations along country roads always remind me of Caddy. I feel like she's somewhere out in the long grass behind the garage. Waiting for a boy. Tossing her hair, and whining with anxiety. She doesn't care about being seen. She just wants to be wanted.

Avatar in Pink: Thirteen Manifestations of Jayne Mansfield

Jessica Melusine

I.

Invoke her and she will come, the holy lurid pink-pierced heart priestess of the Year One shimmying in with a boop-boop-e-doop, forcing milk bottles to spurt their contents skyward, this is her power, this is her birthright, she is the bombshell at the heart of the pentagram, the sex that forces men to their knees, wrapped around her finger as she giggles like a little girl. *Oh my*, she says, astride her seven-headed beast as Los Angeles burns in a Nathaniel West apocalypse, *did I do that?* and laughs because she knows it's true.

II.

Once upon a time, a princess lived in The Pink Palace in Hollywood with Mr. Universe, her beautiful blonde children and her tiny pet dogs. Everything in the house was pink, the champagne, the carpet, her satin dresses, like marshmallows or Hansel and Gretel's candy house and she had a pool in which she swam that said "I love you, Jaynie" at the bottom and that was how she was eternally a virgin, renewed by those holy waters.

But the princess was desirous of knowledge and went forth from her palace to seek it.

III.

Symbology: Hearts and roses, pentagrams.
Attributes: Hearts and roses link her to Erzulie Frieda Dahomey, also

manifest as Erzulie Danto, the Black Madonna. As such, she is linked to the Mater Dolorosa, pictured with piles of pierced and golden hearts. Possible manifestations and her satanic connections also link her to PombaGira, the goddess of whores, artists, bohemians, gay men, and others outside polite society, but a substantial link has yet to be confirmed. May also be associated with the Whore of Babylon, avatar of the Apocalypse.

Colours: Always pink.

Offerings: Pink champagne, cigarettes, perfume, candy, roses, rhinestone jewelry.

Consorts: Mr. Universe, The Black Pope, John F. Kennedy, and others (see cross-reference to Kennedy under *King, Sacred*). Devotees hiss at the name Sam Brody, who dragged the Goddess to the Underworld on the road to New Orleans.

Names: Miss One For The Road, Miss Photoflash, Miss Freeway, Miss Fire Prevention Week, Miss Tomato, Miss 4th of July, Miss Nylon Sweater, Queen of the Aeon, the High Priestess, Playboy's Valentine Girl.

Feast Day: June 29th.

IV.

Vera Jayne Palmer — hardly a name for a movie star. She took the name Mansfield from her husband of four months because it had more panache, attributed the *y* in Jayne to an "unforgettable party at Yale" with a giggle. *Jayne Outpoints Jayne!* the papers clamored at the premiere of *Underwater*, when in a gesture of proto-Bitchcraft, delicate pink-lacquered fingertips unhooked a bikini top and ooooops! Score one for the dumb blonde, minus one for Jane Russell. *What's that girl's name?* reporters clamored, and she rose from the water like Venus herself, ready for questions, ready for her revelation.

What name do you wish? whispers the hooded man in black years later, a dagger held to her throat, she stripped barer than she ever was for *Playboy*. The words fall from her lips and are written in the Devil's Book and Miss Vera Jayne Palmer, Miss Hot Dog Ambassador, Miss 100% Pure Maple Syrup, Miss Geiger Counter has yet another name.

V.

At the height of her popularity, Mansfield sold bottles of her bath water for ten dollars.

VI.

She is a High Priestess now, and that is something to think about and she *will* worry that pretty little head of hers. There's a responsibility and a consciousness; a realization, much like the one that she would one day be famous, that the real power rests in her pink heart, between her pink gates, in the glittered radiance she bestows. Perhaps she read *The White Goddess* and tarted it up in satin, rhinestones, and perfume, perhaps her Hercules put on a bra and panties and made her laugh while as Omphale, she rested beside the pool with a glass of pink champagne.

This is it, she thinks, jerked back to when the final words are spoken, when the anointing is over. *This is Year One.*

VII.

When the Pink Palace was leveled in 2002 to make way for two new mansions, fans crept in and took pictures and pieces of tile from the heart-shaped pool. The tile is scanned and posted on the Internet, cracked and aqua-blue, an object of devotion.

VIII.

"Deep inside every woman there are certain devices designed to attract a man — devices to attract a man's eyes to what he should be attracted to. I've always sensed this — been aware of it in my dress and the way I walk. Well, in this strip I do, I have a perfect chance to attract men's eyes — so I want to be just right. I guess it's a challenge." — Jayne Mansfield (*Adam*, vol. 7, no. 8, 1963)

"If you know how to imitate the woman a man carries within himself, you may have anything you wish that another human can supply." — Anton LaVey, *The Satanic Witch*

IX.

A Lesson in Gematria
IQ: 163
Measurements: 40-21-35
Age at death: 34

X.

The fact remains: Sam Brody was not a good man to our Priestess (*hissssssss!*) and as the Black Pope tells it, Jayne came to him in tears, begging for the life of her children and herself (her son, mauled by a lion whose jaws she could not stop), to save her, save her from Brody. He dried her tears, reminded her of her own power, and told Brody he would be dead within a year. But a love goddess, even fallen on hard times, just can't give up, *the Goddess refuses no man*, and it was with him that she died, crushed under a truck, broken, blonde, and bloodied while miles away, the Black Pope, snipping photos for a scrapbook, noticed in horror his scissors had sliced across her milk-white neck. In San Francisco, after the call, he wept even as he played *Let a Smile Be Your Umbrella*, thinking of the Pink Priestess.

Of course, the story of the Divine does not end with death.

XI.

See Jayne Mansfield's Death Car . . . learn the truth!
Other relics scanned on the web include fabric from the seats of her death car. They are highly sought after by true believers.

XII.

Reborn of the seed of countless emissions of horny men, *ah, ah, ah,* the devotional mana from teenagers staring at her death car and murmuring prayers, the gasp of those who saw her as the Valentine in their father's Playboy magazines, she takes shape as the Whore at the End of The World. *All this for little old me?* she giggles, spinning the pink rhinestone pentagram through her dainty fingers, barebreasted and shameless to her worshippers, watching her power rise, invoked through the rebirth of burlesque and silicon, bleach fumes and wigs and a thousand prayerful wishes from the women who used to kiss the hem of her gown at supper clubs, she ascends and takes her place amid the True Saints, the ones who aren't too high up to hear a prayer or too high up to help a curse.

Ooooooh! she says, stretching out a hand ringed with diamonds, full of power, exalting in her joy, her potency, her apotheosis, *I'm a big girl now!*

XIII.

Jayne Mansfield
1933-1967
We Live to Love You More Each Day

She Pouts Like Scarlett O'Hara

Lenelle Moïse

The dramatic literature professor I am trying to confide in – who is as slim, pale, and pretty as a crisp cigarette – stares at me doe-eyed, as if caught between sunny shock and blinding betrayal. She crosses and uncrosses her candlestick legs; she bites her slight and painted bottom lip; she makes me sick and turns me on as she absentmindedly bounces in the seat of her padded swivel chair, quietly repeating, "I just can't believe it."

I think she wants to point at me; I think I'm entertaining her. I think to offer her popcorn as she leans from the edge of her seat, her eyes glued to the new salty streaks on my cheeks like they're an unpredictable plot twist in a tragic movie on Lifetime. I have just burst into this woman's office, and because I have burst into tears, her concept bubble of an invariably fearless Black Woman has ruptured.

This is my life: I'm a senior at a predominantly white, upper-middle-class, private liberal arts college in upstate New York. I grew up in the projects, in a relatively progressive, socio-economically diverse city outside of Boston. When I talk on the phone with old friends from back home, they inevitably ask, through giggles, "So, how's life in Cow Town?" at which point I sigh.

Life in Cow Town sometimes sucks.

Life in Cow Town means playing the role of the Angry and Invincible Black Bitch – for credit; it means avoiding white students – for my sanity; it means I keep frustrating debates about the intersection (and prevalence) of racism, classism, and sexism limited to the sociology classroom. Life in Cow Town means that when my peers deny their privilege, I make the best of my own: scholarships, odd jobs, and looming loans help sustain me here. I do work hard, but I am lucky.

Life in Cow Town forces a sort of centeredness, too. I have good humour, good grades, strong posture; a tight circle of women of colour, queer folks, and Jewish poets to kvetch with. I'm an out feminist lesbian with a solid live-in girlfriend; I'm a quirky performance artist, and not exactly *the only one.*

Many of my professors are my friends. When we chuckle together about the awkward irony of ending up here in Cow Town, I am either fierce and concise or shrugging with my words.

Today, however — through trembling, chapped lips — my sentences are urgent, circular, and sloppy. I feel especially overwhelmed by my irregular periods, two overdue term papers, and three rejection letters from grad schools I really wanted to attend. I'm trying to tell this white woman — my professor, my friend — that I'm afraid I won't be able to fully participate in our class discussion next period about *'Tis a Pity She's a Whore.*

"I know this is unusual but I'm not feeling particularly focused and I'm afraid that if I start speaking, I'll start balling like I am now." I spill all of this, then pause, taking in her disbelief and the window behind her, a coveted view of the quad. "Things are . . . kind of . . . falling apart for me," I continue, murmuring, hearing the bruises in my voice. "I hope I don't sound too neurotic or stupid."

I couldn't sound as stupid as her. "I just never would have guessed," she starts, smoothing her silk blouse with long, feminine fingers. "I mean, you've always seemed so well put together, so self-assured." She scans the heap of hypersensitivity sitting across from her: me choked up, sweaty and chubby with three wool sweaters to keep out the winter. There is a snowstorm outside.

She avoids direct eye contact, but I sense her blue eyes tiptoe on my skin. She clears her throat, straightens herself, and offers me a tissue. "Forgive me if I seem a bit taken aback. I've just always admired your strength." She almost sounds indignant.

I roll my eyes and bite the soft flesh on the inside of my cheek. I let my heart wander . . . to American Legion Highway, the first public housing complex my mother moved us into, fresh from a separation from my adulterous father. While the sun burned, she supported us by scrubbing toilets at the Hyatt; while the moon hid behind clouds, she trained to be a medical assistant. She was in her early twenties, full of energy, sass, and hope. I was six years old, fragile but friendly. We were on welfare, living in the first apartment she could afford without a cheating man's income.

American Legion Highway — with its mocking, patriotic name — stood across the street from the famous Franklin Park Zoo, which most of its residents could not afford admission to. American Legion Highway was under some god's right foot; the ghetto — a maze of neglected three-storey buildings made of decaying red brick. Black folks settled there and lingered, sometimes for generations. Pizza boys would not deliver to us.

Although it was rarely explicitly uttered, my mother strongly communicated to me that this American Legion Highway was simply where we lived; it was not safe, it was not home. Her rusty blue car barely functioned, but she got an alarm for it anyway. In spite of the fact that the nearest public school was just a block away, Mom struggled to pay nuns at a distant Catholic institution to teach me division, multiplication, manners.

I was also never allowed to play outside. Since we didn't own a working television, this meant lots of after-school time alone reading books, writing juvenile poems, navel-gazing, and hours spent staring out of windows into the mysterious, eerie dark noise of the projects, of the Highway.

One summer Sunday, my father showed up without warning. My mother must have panicked (or wanted to scream at him without my overhearing) because, much to my delight, she blurted out to me, "Go outside!"

This was my life:
Sheltered and naïve, I eagerly run out to meet the now suddenly accessible American Legion Highway kids; kids who quietly watch me morning after morning when I leave my apartment in clean, crisply ironed navy-blue uniforms (which I hate to wear, which my mother can barely afford); kids who see me slide into my seat in the van of a Haitian man my mother collects pennies to pay to drive me to school; unkempt kids who see my brightly decorated, braided, greased black hair, my pouffy, colourful weekend-for-church clothes; American kids who never smile back when I manage to flash my teeth despite my Haitian mother's hand in mine, pulling me along behind, rushing me by their beautiful, rugged, grayish-brown, blank faces.

After months of finding creative ways to talk to myself, I go outside to play in the cement courtyard – like a normal child – with the American Legion Highway kids. Things are going all right for the first few minutes. I notice the boys playing a rough, hoop-less game of basketball and decide to approach the calmer-looking group of girls gathered in a circle instead. A couple of them recognize me instantly and offer tentative hellos. Another even tells me her name.

But the tallest and thickest girl doesn't even blink at my arrival. She simply announces, "I feel like fighting today." Then goes on – as if she didn't say it – to forcefully grind chalk into the small red bucket she holds like a trophy.

"What's she doing?" I ask Name-Girl.

"Making crack," she replies, matter-of-factly. I nod like, duh, like of course I know what this crack thing is.

Tall-Thick shouts like a shameless, seasoned street vendor. "Crack here, people. Get your real crack right here." Project residents of all ages snap their heads back in her direction. Some shrug, some suck their teeth, some gossip on, ignoring; some tell her to shut the fuck up, some laugh at her, aloud.

I just stare, awestruck, and want, immediately – maybe to be like her: so confident and commanding. So certain. So hard.

Tall-Thick catches my eyes and expertly rolls hers. She sticks an index finger into the bucket and points the white in her nail right at me. "Want some crack?" she croons. All the other little girls stiffen, avoid my eyes.

"Um, no thanks," I shrug. "But it looks real good."

"What did you say to me?" she hollers.

I jump, then cringe. "Nothing . . . uh . . . " But before I can bolt, the red bucket clanks ugly against the pavement. Tall-Thick rushes me and I fall back.

stomach socked/ face
stomped on/ rage
repeated/ pounds
precise/ yanks and yells
drowning.

The other girls surround, do not join in, but cheer her on. None of the adults who watch intervene.

there is no sun
just shiny beautiful
brown/ brown
skin/ gnashed
teeth and red
and fist and ground
and fist and she
smells
like bubble-gum and fire
and sweat, lye, and maybe
under all of this
hate/ maybe
she smells like love.

"Fight me, you punk, fight me," she says, and I would but I don't know how to fight. I have never fought before. And I want – to maybe be like her.

"Bor-ing!" Tall-Thick finally spits, and slides off my small, curled-up body. The crowd is silent and I squirm away fast, but limping, to my Mommy.

When the door is answered, I am hysterical – hiccupping too, and hunched over. My parents plead for me to tell them what, who, but my left eye twitches, my little chin trembles, and I can barely get a word out.

My mother marches outside to inquire and scream. My father washes my face and repeats, "What's wrong?" When Mommy returns she tells Father, evenly, that the little girls outside beat me up.

"Did you hit them back?" he asks.

"No," I say, still sobbing, but quite proud of myself.

His body deflates like a punctured balloon, then sharply shoots up like a jack-in-the-box. "You didn't fight back?"

I hesitate. My mother is also appalled.

They sigh and ask almost simultaneously, "Did you let them see you cry?" I start to cry. Mommy kneels and leans her wrinkled forehead to my swollen forehead. Her shoulders soften as she whispers, "Honey, you've got to defend yourself."

My father groans in the background. "I can't believe this daughter of mine – so weak!"

I sink into my skin, feeling pale – not like Tall-Thick – so weak.

We left American Legion Highway for cleaner projects in a wealthier town. I was careful not to let them ever see me cry again — the girls who rejected, the boys who teased, the friends who bit and betrayed; the ones I kissed who never returned calls; homophobic strangers in the park who hurled "sinner" at my soul, then handed out Christian pamphlets.

Once, when a stocky, sarcastic white boy (who swore I was his best friend) casually called me "spear-chucker" in a well-trafficked high school hallway, my heart broke, but like a reflex, I plainly gave him the finger. Later, his idiosyncrasies and secrets eased their way into my short stories. I self-published those stories and distributed copies to passersby in that same well-trafficked hallway. He cried.

Revenge tasted sweet, then dissolved.

Daily acts of violation, small spiritual assaults — being followed for having brown skin in a pastel-themed boutique, catcalls — these things never ceased. Later, I learned to write bitingly eloquent letters, which were designed to make the reader — my abusers — feel small. Later, too — still biting — I recited love poems on Cow Town stages, and those who once threw pamphlets, threw praise.

Tears streamed — always — but only under covers, in closets, leaning against bad graffiti in small public restroom stalls; tears streamed — always — but only behind locked doors. If ever I felt myself coming undone, even in front of lovers and close friends, I silently chanted: I'm capable. I'm self-possessed (Papi, see). I'm a Strong Black Woman (Mommy, look). I take care of myself. I stand tall, thick-skinned. I am hard.

But this is my life: unreleased hurt adds up. The body breaks out and breaks down. And now, I sit across from an older woman who, in order to revere me, has rendered me mythical. For her inspiration — against my humanity — she treats me as though my blood-shot, pleading eyes are evidence of the fraud I've been all along. She treats me as though I've lied to her about my hard-earned strength, because here I am — finally — admitting a moment of weakness.

"I just can't believe it," my professor repeats. I feel certain that she weeps sometimes, as I do. And despite this, I feel certain she needs me to be what she is not: magical and irrepressible, statically mighty and ever-loud, discarnate and invulnerable. *Fight me, you punk, fight me* — she says it without saying — but I do not want to fight. I swallow my disappointment before it swells into rage, which is what, after all, would appease her. I decide I am not safe here, I am not home; I cannot lay my burden here; I will choose not to fight this battle.

I sniff up; manage a gallant grin to make pleasant and passive my aggression. "You know what?" I say, rising from my chair, "I think I am overreacting. I think I have PMS."

Die-hard feminist that this white woman is, my last statement makes her wince. "Don't be ridiculous," she protests, but I wink like Hattie McDaniel, so she pouts like Scarlett O'Hara. Her door slams behind me.

This is my dream:
I peel off three sweaters, discard my scarf and boots, and step out onto the snow-struck quad, into the cold, bleak day. Frozen flakes of ice conspire with a sharp northern wind to whip my shivering chin. I squat just beneath a woman's office window. I do not call her name, but I love her.

Rocking from heel to toe, I hold two bare, brown hands up to the white, white sky. I open my mouth and wail:

I am afraid everyday,
many times a day. I cannot fly,
witchly or transcendent, above
my fear and pain. I weep for little girls –
the one I was, the one I could not be.
I am myself and human.

My quivering tongue recycles this fresh chant. And though my eyes are puffy, throbbing, and half-shut, I feel women gathering – circling – around me.

They do not point, they do not laugh; they do not stay silent. We know each other, after all; we've seen each other around. One of them loves me back.

Red Light

Anna Camilleri

So, why is it that a red light means STOP,

and a red dress means GO?

No one stumbles out of bed
and into a red dress.

A red dress is never casual.

Imagine it there.
Do you see it?

Is it folded?
Hanging tight by
spaghetti straps?
Is it silk, cut on
the bias, plunging
neckline?

Is it on a mannequin
in a department
store window?
Or is it on the
body of a woman?

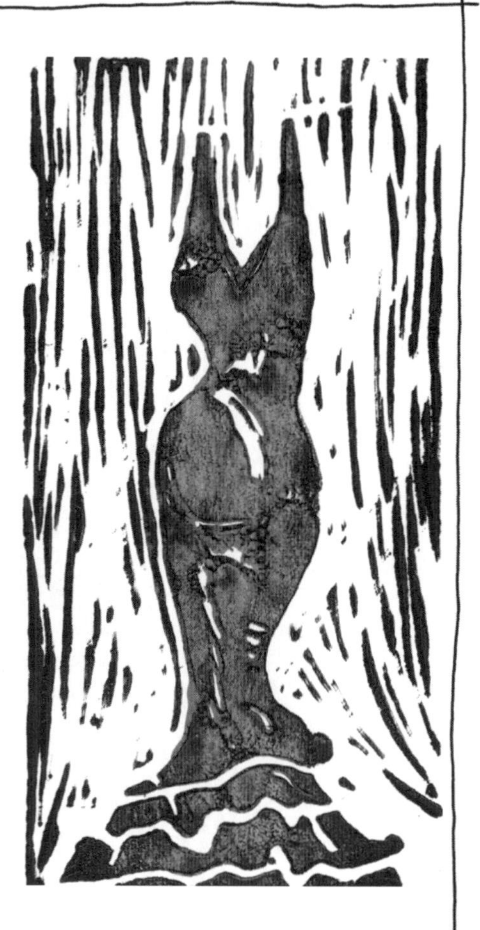

Is she the object or is
the **dress**?

The fantasy, LADY IN RED, is not mine.

Her head tilted just so, waiting for a strong arm to propel her forward into animation, like a blow-up doll. Waiting for a hot tongue moving hot air. Waiting to have the red stuffed right out of her. To be cruise-controlled into the centre of her cavernous self. To be fucked into OBLIVION.

That fantasy is not mine.

I remember being a girl. Eyes like stars falling, big hair bundled like celery. When I was hurting, I imagined a woman in a red dress.

And I wondered what she would do in my place.

She became a muse
in my life, as real
as anything.

An angel.
A siren.
Shining a light
in the dark corners.

Everything She Asks of Me

Daphne Gottlieb

So, I'm dating Marilyn Monroe. We're living together, actually. Right now, she's sitting on the white couch with the black stains, watching me write this. *What are you writing?* she wants to know. *A love letter,* I say.

She's eating grapes. She's really into them right now. One by one, she sucks them into her mouth with a little pop, crushes them between the whitest of teeth with the gentlest of violence. *What's the opposite of fruit?* she wants to know.

I don't know, I say. *Meat?* She purses her lips, considering. *No,* she says. *I don't think there is an opposite of fruit.*

We are both girls, which is true, but it's like saying that a nectarine and a watermelon are both fruit. She's a little tart rolling over the tongue, creamy; I crumble in the mouth, wet and rough.

She skips over to the bed, almost invisible with her cream skin on cream satin, hair the colour of headlights at night. *Do these sheets make me look fat?* she asks. She's serious. *How do you know if you're beautiful? Are you only beautiful if someone else thinks you are? And what does it cost?* She almost only ever speaks in questions.

Last week, she was obsessed with cantaloupe and Eartha Kitt. As I got ready for work, she jumped up and down on the bed, singing, *I Wanna Be Evil.* When I came home, she'd tried to dye her hair black. The dye was spattered on the walls, the couch, the floor, sticking to everything but her hair, which shone like a canary in a coal mine. *It didn't work right, huh,* she asks. *Do you hate it?* Her face crumples. *I hate it,* she says. I rubbed toothpaste on her hair until it was back to blonde, and we ate cantaloupe in bed, gently scooping the cool, calm flesh into our mouths.

Stop writing. Come talk to me, she says.

Okay.

It's hard being dead, she says. *I never look any older. I want to know what I really look like.*

I can't fix it for you, I tell her. *I think that this is love but it feels just like helplessness,* I say.

What is the opposite of helplessness? she asks. *What is the cost of death?* She takes the phone off the hook. A recording plays: *If you'd like to make a call, please —* she wants to know, *if you leave a phone off the hook, how long does the busy signal sound before the line goes dead?* She drops the phone receiver on the bed. *Is there a time limit to how long you can be happy for?* The phone blares its staccato call through the twilight. *This is always the last thing I ever hear,* she says, as we taste the fruit and meat of each other's mouths, as I dissolve into her kiss.

Doña Julia

Sharon Bridgforth

she had a red v-neck sheath dress/on
that clung
like a wise man begging for mercy.
her wide
wide hips
pulled the tight tight dress/up
a little
showing more of the seam running down
the back of her skin-toned Black black-stockinged legs
her red pumps glittering a good match to the veil blowing round her
wide red red brimmed hat which matched her clutch bag
and fingernails.
she strolled up the way like wasn't nobody around/like she window
shopping on a breezy day/like she under magnolias and moonlight/like
she carrying some
voodoo ass to a long anticipated date.
this was doña julia
and when she got all the way up the walk up the stairs up front and centre

she swung down and/slapped
the good rev little clean out his pulpit seat.
doña julia then hiked that red dress up up and put a glittering red pump
down each side the good reverend little
like she doing a merengue.
after she got her standing/straddle just
right over the good reverend little
doña julia say

mafucka
i tole you
to leave
her
alone!

doña julia then pulled a blade from her red red
clutch bag and
ssssssslash
the good reverend little from this life to the next.
doña julia unstraddle/straighten she titties
turn
toss her hat off
then
let her long thick Black black curls fall into a wild release down the back
of her tight tight red red dress as she
strolled
back down the stairs down the walk
out the double doors
into the bursting sunlight.

Violent Collections, Anxious Supplements

Lisa Foad

Violent Collections

On my way into work, the black-lettered byline touts, RED HOT EROTIC NUDE LIVE! UNCENSORED VIP COUCH DANCING. WELCOME MOLSON INDY FANS. Gold-plated brick exterior, a pocketful of cascading neon stars, and a girl — she lights up one leg at a time.

Working hard to keep you hard, says the DJ.

ABSOLUTELY NO TOUCHING: $10,000 FINE, says the sign at the back of the bar. It's nestled between a plastic potted plant and a cylindrical aquarium bearing floating faux fish.

En route to the change room, the baby blue hallway walls are littered with sloppily stenciled metallic stars. Gold and silver. Chipped tips. And housed within the belly of each star, a name: Misty. Sapphire. Jasmyn. Jewel. Justice. Nikki. Bubble letters, i's dotted with hearts.

And we are a sky and the sky is the limit.

My back is always straight. My skin is always snowy. My lips are always dewy. And my nipples are always hard. I always lean in. My legs move in pieces. My back arches perfectly. I bend over with aplomb. The winged blades of my shoulders ache from feelings like flying. My spine is a beacon. Each vertebra whispers and clicks open, clicks shut, like 33 doors or memories or ongoing moments, indecisive tulips blooming, then retreating.

I am a topographical wonder. Intonation, incantation, intoxication.

Revealing everything and nothing.

And at work, a customer says, *You have found yourself a fan.*

I keep their business cards. Vice President of Sales. CEO. Model & Talent Scout. I slip them into my purse along with fistfuls of $20s. I tell myself that one day I'll make art out of these slim slips of cardstock. An intricately imbricated mosaic, alternately glossy and matte, minimal and garish, proffering mythological certainties – perimeters, locular inhabitability, things I think I know, like the simplicity of a clean break. There are no such separations. Only pools of space.

The graffiti on the brick wall outside my bedroom window says, BOY BANDS SUCK. GIRLS SUCK BETTER. TITS RULE. And when I wake, I want – new shoes, an espresso.

The sign outside of the church I pass on my way to Dufferin Station says, FREEDOM FROM TEMPTATION. THE RIGHTEOUS WILL NOT GO HUNGRY. In my palms I hold the freedom to starve.

A sandwich board on the sidewalk en route to the thrift store promises AID TO WOMEN. My friend Lil tells me it's an abortion clinic, kept quiet to avoid protests. When I ask how she's sure, she pauses and says, *The protestors.* There is some debate, however. Rumour has it that the abortion clinic is a few doors down, that in fact the AID TO WOMEN is a Christian offering for ladies who don't know any better. And Maggie's, support for sex workers, is located on the same small stretch of real estate. Here on this corner, the options for women in need are endless. I wonder, if I stand on this corner long enough, will I get confused? Lose my bearings? Will I default, revert, become amnesiac? Will I opt for salvation? Seek redemption? A rest? And suddenly every step is suspect and every suspect is a door.

When I was six, my aunt took me downtown. I waited outside while she went into a store. When she came out she scolded me. *Hasn't your mother taught you anything? Don't stand still. You'll look like a hooker.* She taught me how to pace sidewalks with certainty, to always look like I had somewhere to go, even if it was just in circles. Now when I walk, it's with purpose, but for different reasons. In the midst of any Q&A, salutation, signature, exchange, I anticipate the catch.

Hesitation has gotten me nowhere. And I can only think in bullets, a string of directives:
Eat, or you'll faint.
Hail the first cab you see.
Don't talk to strangers.
Invisible deodorant does not glow in black light.

And these are the spaces that make framing and composition possible. This is the sky, and the sky is the limit. And I love the way my hair falls across my eyes the most.

I carry a purse that doubles as a suitcase. And when I inhale, it is sharp.

Anxious Supplements

Vitamins.
Pills.
Vitamins.
Pills.
B-12 and rosehips, iron and ginseng. I take two in the morning, two at night.
I carry hand sanitizer, a sewing kit, oxygen mask, a quarter.
I keep my ID on me at all times. Check it for accuracy, regularly.
Thread my keys between my fingers, ready.

At home, I twist the locks, secure the windows, draw the curtains, turn out the lights and sit quietly. I wonder, can anyone hear me? I make hot chocolate with milk, not water, but let it cool and crust, ignored. Posturing the art of comfort. Instead, I numb my lips and tongue with Listerine. Rub my shoulder where the bone sticks out. Run my tongue along my gums. Check for a dial tone, a pulse, and call someone. I'll call anyone.

And at work, a customer says, *Come back to Chicago with me. I'll take care of everything.*

And I keep everything. Save everything.

Old cassette tapes, airplane vomit bags, keys that no longer open anything, love letters. A handheld alarm and a giant safety pin with which to alternately deafen and prick potential attackers, both city-specific gifts from my grandmother. Sometimes I tuck my hair behind my ears, furrow my brow, and attempt to dispose of the notion that sentiments are housed in objects. These nostalgic returns yield nothing, no thing.

The giant heart-shaped crystal bowl from my sister is not my sister.

It's not even an adequate representation of her — she despises decorative ornamentation and avoids glassware. She fears spontaneous cracks, wayward shards, and puncture wounds. Unleashed dogs and expired yogurt. That something completely unrelated but extreme and tragic will happen to someone she loves. Plastic cups and avoiding streets that start with the letters J and S are preventative measures.

Today on the phone she tells me that I am irrational, that I can't keep saving things.

I take out the trash. Return the empties. Bleach my hair. I try to write, resisting the urge to merely record. Instead I pen my name in blue ink, house it in the belly of a star. Chain-smoke. Read my horoscope. It says, *Watch for clues.*

And later, in the midst of throwing out the giant heart-shaped crystal bowl that is not my sister, I stumble, fall, and accidentally slit my wrist with a wayward shard of glass. I bandage the wound with toilet paper and Scotch tape, but it bleeds profusely through the tissue. The gash is shallow, horizontal, and somewhat humiliating, in that *Don't want to go, just want to show* way.

I have never been superstitious. I have always been superstitious. I cry for help. Try to be a good friend. And wonder things like, which room do I look best in?

At work, everyone looks good, even the floating fake fish. We are black-lit heartbeats, legs moving in pieces.

And at work, a customer says, *You don't belong here. You've got class. I could take you anywhere.*

He means, *Without you, I can't belong here.*

We are antithetical desiring machines writing a story of need. Mine is written through red bills and green bills and pink-lipped armour. Amour. His is written through this girl and that girl, working hard to keep him hard. Impenetrable. Sure. Secure. Like a rock.

Desire is a multi-pronged instrument of restless promise. Promising alleviation. And I am, bruised from the pole, shiny with soft sweat, a vision of potential, capability, culpability. This is the story and it goes on and on.

And at work, a customer says, *I bet you're always horny.*

Though bound by the inevitability of its failure, desire is caught within the arrogant mythology of its capacity for success. And it does not tire.

And, *Hi. Hi. Hi.* I am a double, *Baby*. A triple, *Baby*. I am the supplement, supplanting. I am the insurance, ensuring. That the ontological joke is no joke.

I write notations on their business cards, tiny reminders dated in blue ink. This one wanted me to fly to Philly for the weekend. This one gave me stockings. This one thinks my name is Nicole. This one tried to stick his finger up my ass. This one spent $800. This one bought us champagne. This one brought his wife. All of them say I am different. All of them think they are different. I told them so and so it was. I tell them so and so it is.

I am, in quarters and eighths, the best, the worst.

Boom! Bang! Pow! Kazaam! Without me, there could be no way.

From my purse that doubles as a suitcase, I retrieve a breath mint. Lips and tongue numb. I wonder things like, How many twenties are zipped inside the ankle of my boot? Am I pretty? Will I be saved? And, should the offer present itself, will I remember to refuse?

Apotheosis

I am perfect. I bloom and beam. My shoulders sing. My head tilts with ease. And my legs spread so easily. I am sheer radiance, rosy and fully realized, made up. I lick my lips. I look away. I don't look away. I am a field of flowers. Azaleas. Lilies. Chrysanthemums. Violets. *Pick me. Pick me.*

I play *Snake* on my cell phone, call my girlfriend. Wait for the one. There are several.

And a customer says, *You are the bedrock of beauty.* He likes the blondeness of my hair and the way my body curves like a nation. He is writing a novel, a tribute, to all of the beautiful women in the world, the women who have touched him. Made him mean. He says he will dedicate the first chapter to me.

And without further ado.

Sweetheart. I am leaning on the hood. Digging through the trunk. Staring down vanishing points. This is love. This is not love.

And a customer says, *I know what you want. I can see it in your eyes. You come and come, don't you?*

Baby. I am leaning on his shoulder. Digging through his pockets. Staring down vanishing points. This is love. This is not love.

And a customer says, *I hate to see you pass your body around like a pack of cigarettes. Let me be the one to save you.*

Precious. Three minutes at a time. I can say yes without saying a word.

And, *shhh.* We close our eyes and pretend that these economies of desire have no tangible currency. This is the art of collaboration. The real thing. Everything and nothing.

The one. The only one. I swear, by the powers vested in me. And, *I am so wet.* And are you a believer?

Into my purse that doubles as a suitcase, I slip another business card.

Love Thwarted

I am irreverent, a heart bent on refusal. I refuse to wear spandex. I slip purloined suggestions like notes under my tongue, mouth the words, let them dissolve. I'm not always sure of the things that spill out of me. Want, wherewithal, weeks and weeks of need. But I am a girl with stamina and resolve. This is a violent housing, but I am a violent collection. I rub things out, tug on other people's hair, slam doors, eat larger portions.

And at work, a customer says, *I want to see you come.*

He means, *I need proof.* Testimony. Evidence.

And in the privacy of the darkened VIP lounge, he is sunk low on the leatherette love seat; I promise and deny, promise and deny — *jouissance*!

For here, something is always missing.

The mark.
The matter.
The *Boom! Bang! Pow! Kazaam!*
Suggesting the all that he can be. The all that we can be.

Suddenly, the necessity of faith is tabled like no tomorrow. Are you a believer?

I finger my dress, pick off another sequin. It's mostly sheer now except for the sides, the parts that never rub off.

And into my purse that doubles as a suitcase, I slip the sequin and another business card.

Later, at home, my roommate and I are interrupted by a faint whining or humming or sighing.

What's that noise? I ask.

Adjusting her cap, hands in the fridge, she says, *What noise?*

Eating licorice, I say, *Don't you hear that?*

We perch quietly in the kitchen, waiting for clues.

I think it's a car alarm, she says. Slams the fridge shut with her hip, a mango in each hand.

Ohhh, I nod. Dig an apple out of the fruit bowl. And discover the handheld alarm from my grandmother, whining and humming and sighing.

Victory Girl

Darryl Berger

early rounds

Victory's early fortunes rise and fall with her parents. Her mother is constant, smiling close up, an abstraction of buoyancy and light. Her father Earl is removed, elusive, gravity-seeking at the corner of things, somehow more important. He is a semi-successful boxer — semi-successful because he likes to drink. Actually, he loves it. Dreams for it. When he can't drink, when he is training and suffering and the dreaming is deepest, he goes around slamming doors.

After a doomed title shot (the champion, a Korean, cunningly uses his face to break Earl's right hand), he retires, buys a house along the coast. At the top of a hill, overlooking the ocean, it is perfect in its height and whiteness and opacity all around. Victory loves it there, *location location location* she hears on the television one day, it makes such perfect sense, everyone wants to be near water. Swimming makes Victory ache, ache inside to swim all the time, later in memory she is a little girl swimming in rapture, immersed in the fluid magic of sparkling vastness that God calls the ocean. *The ocean is my motion*, she hears that somewhere too, sings it to herself in beamy loops. Victory is a good swimmer, sleek and efficient, her mouth drinks air like it's the future; when her stomach hurts (only sometimes) she turns over on her back, straightens out thin and divine, packs her eyes with cloud. Victory owns her own movements, feels the force of her will as significant. In the water, she can go anywhere she wants to. Her little sister Pyrrhic stays on the beach, sits with her pad of acid-free paper and paints the same picture over and over again, blue on blue with whirls of white, airy and pretty. Reading one of her books about sticks and coins, their mother says that Fate has given each of them a special talent.

cut

Victory's stomach starts to hurt more and more. Pain comes at her in rushes. A doctor pushes between folds of her skin with two fingers, watches her wince, talks to her mother. Victory goes into the hospital to have her appendix removed. *That was a big one,* the doctor tells Victory afterwards. *Very inflamed.*

Victory's family visits. Pyrrhic brings her paintings, new ones with touches of fire red in a swirling sky, the paper curled at the edges. Visiting hours are over at eight o'clock. On the drive home one night her dad is mesmerized by a passing car, by the sight of two little Asian girls crowding their heads out the window, laughing into the open air. He swerves into them. Both cars careen off the road, jumping like angry beetles.

judges

The funeral is poorly attended. Some mob types are there, smelling like cigarettes. They have money and damp hands.

corner

Victory goes to live with her aunt in Saskatoon, Saskatchewan. It is a small city in the middle of a flat, dry place. It is a city full of practical, modest people who make common leaps of false logic. Victory loathes them. She tries tarot cards, extended bouts of staring and willing. But the ocean remains long gone.

Her aunt is severely single. She has a wide array of rules and expectations of the detailed, insignificant sort, the ordered life with no plan. She teaches Victory how to clean things properly (properly!), but dust is a persistent enemy. With puberty Victory puts on weight, grows sullen. Her only friend Roxanne sees this, asks indulgently how it is to live there.

It makes me hungry, Victory replies. Victory skips her high school graduation to move into a tiny corner suite at the top of a four-storey building downtown. There are no skyscrapers in a city like this.

trainers

Victory and Roxanne get jobs at the same office. They process data. They are at the bottom of the white-collar world where everyone wears clean clothes. *You girls run this place, you know,* their supervisor says, staring at their tits.

stick and move

Victory watches the news. Standing before bodies of Islamic insurgents, a government official in Tajikistan explains, through a sheen of sweat and slipping smile, that violence just happens, *violence just happens in a dynamic society.* Victory likes the roominess of the answer. Any explanation is appreciated. It's better than nothing, better than just sitting there stuffing handfuls of Cheerios into her mouth. When a Russian submarine lies powerless at the bottom of the Bering Sea, Victory dreams of a giant fish with metal skin gently dying in mid-swim.

weigh-in

Victory and Roxanne try a new diet: fat-burning soup. Three cups of V8 juice, one carrot, three or four green onions, one can of tomatoes, one-half head of cabbage, one can of green beans, one green pepper, five stalks of celery, one package of soup mix, one cube of bouillon, two cups of water. Chop up the vegetables. Add everything into a pot. Mix. Boil quickly. After ten minutes, turn down the heat to simmer, keep stirring until all the vegetables are tender.

There is a seven-day regimen that follows, the only constant being the consumption of soup. On Day One you also get to eat fruit – cantaloupe and watermelon being lowest in calories and therefore best. At the end of Day Two is the reward of a baked potato (with butter). Day Three is more fruit. Day Four, hump day, brings bananas and skim milk. For Day Five you can choose between ten to twenty ounces of beef or up to six fresh tomatoes. Day Six is beef and vegetables day, all you want. And on Day Seven you get brown rice, unsweetened fruit juice, and more vegetables. *Congratulations*, the recipe reads, *you just lost ten to fifteen pounds.*

Yet Victory's recipe reads somewhat differently. Day One and Two run well enough, promises and appeals and afternoon stomach-kneading seeing her through. She can imagine melting away. But Day Three is sick with the simmering affliction of soup, the taste of it, its blandness and vile texture. A salad comes as recompense, still healthy, but then the Italian dressing. The full implosion always arrives on Day Four, fast-food never tasting so good, so damned good, while the soup sits despised in the fridge, a false prophet. There is never a Day Five.

body blow

Victory squints to see it, screwing her face up disdainfully. The sun sits pulsing in the sky against her, perfect and triumphant in its clean sheet of cloudless blue. This, after she prayed so hard for rain. *Just one little storm*, she had prayed, staring down at The Tower.

The company barbecue is fifty or so people navigating the front lawn of the office building with paper plates and inappropriate shoes. Gathering in clusters. Roxanne is not among them, having phoned in sick to go shopping for clothes, having lost thirty pounds from the fat-burning soup, boundless energy and interest in everything now, posture and hair products and especially clothes, their colours and combinations. Victory stands off to the side, alone, not even tasting her third hamburger, a blocky shape against the heat, her insides boiling against her, seething at herself, at every one of her two hundred and thirty-three pounds, desperately hating everyone.

jab

Victory comes home to messages that are not for her, someone's elderly mother pleading *Please call, we haven't heard from you in such a long time.* The messages themselves don't bother Victory so much as the disappointed, disembodied muttering at the end when the old woman hands the phone back to her husband to hang up on the wall.

clinch

A rocket named Mariana explodes on the launch pad in the jungles of French Guyana. A nine-year-old Scottish girl who is allergic to water has her specially-designed raincoat stolen in a home burglary. After a televised appeal from her parents, the coat is anonymously returned but the thieves have shredded it. Flooding and mud slides in Venezuela kill tens of thousands. A massive cyclone wrecks Bangladesh. Iran is devastated by an earthquake. There is vicious sectarian violence, widespread rioting and looting in Belfast. A giant tsunami obliterates East Java and Bali. Victory watches it all, fills herself with it. The televised noise of the world sounds like a death-rattle to her ears, and she cheers it.

combinations

Suddenly the weather is surprising, confusing. Inspiring fear. Then it simply stops. All over the globe, all at once, the sky crowds with cloud. Day after day, bit by bit, it fills itself in. Scientists sputter or shake their heads, although one blames teflon. Everything becomes darker and darker.

People are inspired in their bad behaviour. The Shining Path assassinates seven judges in one day. An American congressman murders an intern, then his family, then himself. The Japanese Red Army blows up a NATO conference. India invades Pakistan, then China invades India. The Russian government is angry and menacing, feels left out but consoles itself with exterminating the Chechens. When a teller in Detroit doesn't move fast enough, a robber shoots her and all fourteen other people in the bank. Two nihilistic, love-struck German teenagers kill their parents, a neighbour, a school teacher, a policeman, a postman, and a dog. A man in full Klingon uniform starts shooting at a *Star Trek* convention in Mesquite, Texas, killing eleven before a burly Captain Kirk brains him with a phaser. Ethicists call it mass expressions of degeneracy. Victory stops going to work, eats and sleeps in front of her television.

The sky is falling. Every morning is dimmer. The ceiling of cloud looms lower. It makes you stand and stare. Blankness. People say things like *doomsday* and *end of the world*. They go crazy. The news, while it lasts, is appalling, thrilling. *This is zero-hour for mankind*, the announcer says.

late rounds

The electricity goes out. Then the water.

decision

The sirens have finally stopped. Victory stands on the edge of the roof, arms out, balancing, her feet halfway into the air. There is nothing to see now, the whole world choked by rolling cloud, all around. You can reach out and touch it. The air is heavy and almost silent, only the distant sound of rushing water, you can barely hear it, somewhere close but beyond. One by one, Victory tosses tarot cards into the nothingness. Then she assumes a diver's pose.

the siren's story

Barbara Jane Reyes

she wasn't born in this city. she found its basalt greenstone chunks, seafloor forced skyward. it found her hands through mist and odours whirring pigeons' clubfeet fluttering, toothless men's paper sacks spilling elixirs, roots, shark fin tonics. heat swelling sewer steam rising, side street chess match maneuvers mystifying. it sought her whirlwind hair, grown seavine thick. songbird, adrift, nestling neon, she crafted snares for moths, butterflies, treasure hunting children tracing ideographs: sky, sun. patina spires, smirking dragon boys humming silk lanterns, flight of phoenixes through fish vendors' stalls, corrugated plastic blackbird perches, jade-ringed gardens, needle-tipped shanties. it bulleted trees, lighting hash pipes; herbalists' storefront canopies concealing leathered men, versed in languages of whiskered ghosts. it invented her dialect carving tongue: salt fables, yellow caution tape palaces. she lost herself in this city. it lured her, drank her air; honey voice's precision, hybrid beyond memory. songbird, adrift, this city's misplaced siren. migration patterns subterranean streams swallowed whole.

Yellow Rose of Texas

Bren Simmers

If that show-off from San Antonio hadn't entered at the last minute, Mary Kay Ash would have won the Yellow Rose of Texas beauty contest. Seeing as there were only twenty permanent residents in Hot Wells, Texas, the crown was as good as hers. But then the judges went and opened the running to guests of the hotel – rich folk seeking cures in the pools that smelled of rotten eggs.

Mary Kay spent all morning with her hair curlers in and a prayer on her tongue, reapplying old lipstick that her mother fished out special for weddings and funerals – the cheap stuff that slid off her mouth. She was plain-faced and pious the rest of the time wearing a housedress under her coat; the floral print worn see-through in places. Mary Kay tried to persuade her mother that pink lipstick wasn't becoming for her skin tone – why not a Marion Davies red? *Earl's* had some in stock. They could stop by after church and pick one up.

Waste not, want not, her mother replied, leaving her daughter to beg for samples at San Antonio drugstores, to eavesdrop in beauty salons for tips on how to accentuate her assets – clear skin and wide-set eyes – and how to pencil in fuller lips while remaining faithful to *God first, family second, career third.*

It was the face powder that did her in: discontinued stock, two shades too light, ran down her face in channels of sweat. At the close of the parade, the old men sat smoking their pipes on the hotel veranda, the women paraded out front in their finest dresses, under shade umbrellas. Mary Kay could tell from their faces that she'd lost, how they glanced over her quickly before settling on Lucy in her light green dress, waving like the queen; her face a perfect mask in the fervent Texas heat.

Darla's Goodbye

Alec Butler

From birth, Ma knew I was different, born to make a difference. At family gatherings, Ma bragged about how I painted abstracts on the wall next to the crib with my poo. If she'd known anything about art, we could have jumped the gun on that "piss Christ" artist. Poo Art. Being artistic was a mortal sin where I grew up. Might as well be queer.

I was more than a tomboy. Growing up in Sydney, on Cape Breton Island, Ma never stopped setting people straight when I got taken for her son. She wasn't sure puberty would take care of things, so she took me to doctors all the time. *No worries, Ma, just because I want a dick now doesn't mean I am a dick.*

One Saturday afternoon after *Star Trek*, Ma tried to get me to wear a bra. In class that year, all the girls wore training bras, training their breasts to push up and out. I did not want mine to stick out, did not want to show them off. Even the gang of boys who looked up to me for adventures since I was cut from the clothesline were starting to notice. It was embarrassing.

But Ma was stubborn, she presented the bra to me with a hopeful smile, urging me to take it. "W-w-what's that for," I stammered.

"Look at the size of your breasts, dear. What will people think?"

"I don't care what people think. I don't want it. Take it back."

I ran out into the backyard, slamming the screen door. I took off on my beat-up-banana-seat bike and rode around for hours, trying to imagine another place, a place where birds sang in trees not stunted by pollution, a paradise I glimpsed in dreams, where waves lapped on an imagined shoreline that was not toxic. A place where there were people like me, where people like me could be more than myth.

I was ashamed of my body, ignored the fact that my period had started. There was some kind of mix-up; this wasn't happening to me. I was encouraged by the moustache coming in over my upper lip, fascinated by the peachy down sprouting on my cheeks and chin. I used a pencil not only to write stories and sketch with, but to darken in my beard. Listening through the floorboards to the sounds of Ma and Pa in the kitchen fighting about how to buy groceries and pay the bills on pogey, fighting about what to do about me. Rough nights under the covers with piles of books stuffed under my bed, pouring over stories of goddesses and gods and the double-sexed seer Teresias in the Funk & Wagnall's. I discovered Artemis, the moon goddess, the huntress, my first fierce femme, weaving fantasies where I'm the hero, fighting off monsters while secretly fearing I was one. The battle between Medusa and Perseus fired up my imagination. Escaping under my tent of blankets, flashlight hot in my hand. Stroking the paper under my fingertips like the belly of a lover, tides of blue ink flowed from the tip of my ballpoint pen. At fourteen, I knew this secret vice of writing was a lifeline to paradise. Tales spun through time, space and genders, my parched and grimy world transformed.

But first I had to get through this Hades. My house stood near the slag heap at the edge of the steel plant that roared hellfire night and day. My bedroom window looked out on a slag heap, tar ponds, and smoke stacks. The smell of rotten eggs smothered the street, crept under the covers, burned into our sinuses, made our nights noxious. On the nights when they were dumping the slag, I imagined this was how brimstone stank in hell. In one story I am a resistance fighter in World War II. Among the partisans, I bind my breasts and am taken for a man. Wounded and trapped behind enemy lines, a beautiful resistance fighter discovers my secret while nursing my wounds. She confesses her passion for me and promises to keep my secret. Different from the other stories I wrote, in this one I'm the one who needs saving and she's the one who mows down a dozen Nazis with a machine gun as we make our escape.

I confessed my night time sojourns to Darla, an older girl in art class, sixteen.

In Grade Eight, Ma scraped the money together to send me to art class on the other side of the Overpass every Saturday. Her sacrifice, meant to send me soaring, weighed me down. I couldn't tell Ma how ashamed I was when the other kids called me a *slagger*, how they looked down their noses at my work, my family, my neighbourhood. I heard through the grapevine that Darla thought I was cute. That was all the encouragement I needed. The other kids looked down their noses at Darla too. Because she was a stoner, because she was white trash, they called her a bitch, a slut. They called us both lezzies. It was confusing; I didn't know what a lezzie was. Darla told me to look up an island called Lesbos in the Funk & Wagnall's. It sounded fantastic, but is that where we belonged? I'd never look good in a toga.

Darla stayed out in the bush with her hippie aunt while her mother was in the Butterscotch Palace. Back home that's what we called the loony bin. Her aunt drove her into town in a VW van covered in flowers and peace signs every Saturday. It was the only set of wheels like it for miles around. We'd hang out after class smoking joints at the foot of a pylon under the Overpass while her aunt worked at the co-op bookstore. We shared our hopes and dreams: me, a famous writer, her a famous painter.

One rare sun-blasted day, we were fooling around with a Super-8 camera her aunt's draft dodger boyfriend left behind when he went to work in the gold mines up north. As I was filming her, Darla started playing for the camera. Or was she flirting with me? I can still see how she looked up at me through her long dark lashes, how she laughed and spread her legs wide — the denim of her bellbottoms outlining her pussy lips, her venus mount in high relief. I remember how she touched herself, how she drew me in, pulled me towards her and took my hand, placed it on her soaked denim crotch: "Feel how wet that is."

All I knew was that I was in heaven. I stroked her and she kissed me. The hum of motor engines and the whish of rubber tires on the blacktop above us punctuated her passionate cries. Up against that rusty pylon, she let me rub her off.

"So sweet," she said when she caught her breath. "And you think you're so rough."

She touched herself, laid her fingers on my lips, fragrant with her. "Shhh. I'm not meeting my auntie like this; walk me home."

It was five clicks by road, one click as the crow flies. Darla took me to a path that short-cut through the woods. Before puberty hit, Pa used to take me hunting and fishing with him; I missed being in this cathedral of big trees. And here I was entering this sacred place with Artemis by my side. Halfway down the path, we made out up against a big oak tree. Darla wanted to touch me, but I pushed her hand away.

"Trust me," she said, her voice husky with passion. But I couldn't. Not yet.

Dusk was falling by the time we got to the trailer. Her aunt was sitting in a lawn chair by the wood pile, an axe embedded in a nearby log. She was smoking filterless Export A's and chugging Moosehead. She was pissed. I guess the hippie thing only went so far. Darla shooed me off back down the path from where we came, saying she would see me in class next week.

I was beside myself with worry when Darla didn't show up for art class the week after we had our adventure in the bush, nor in the three weeks that followed. I felt like I'd been kicked out of paradise. When Darla moved back into town with her so-called crazy mother a month later and started going to my school, I was over the moon. I couldn't believe it. The agony of not knowing what was going on over the previous month left the moment I laid eyes on her.

I sent her a note asking her to meet me in the baseball diamond across from school. I waited in the dugout, my heart pounding like a Led

Zeppelin bass line. Through a chainlink fence I watched her walk towards me. Part of me wanted to run away — I'd been ambushed here before and I had the scars to prove it. About ten feet away, she stopped to spark up a joint and I knew it was safe. She looked at me like I was a drink, and boy, was she thirsty. She passed me the joint through the chainlink. I entwined my fingers with hers and squeezed tight. When she touched me everything else became a dream. She looked into my eyes for a long time before she spoke.

"They're watching me like a hawk."

"Let's go away. Go where they can't keep us apart."

"I can't run away anymore. I'm graduating next year. I'm not gonna blow it now."

I knew she was right, but I wanted things to be different. Running away would ruin her plans to get a university scholarship, to escape from this rough place with dignity. But in that moment I had no dignity. I pouted and pleaded.

"I just can't see you anymore. They'll kill you." A tear slid down her cheek as she pulled her hand from mine, blew me a kiss, and turned away.

What really worried Ma when I was a kid was the wanderlust. She had to tie me to the clothesline to keep me from climbing over the fence whenever her back was turned. The lay of the land beyond our backyards was barren and alluring like the surface of the moon. In the summer, neighbourhood kids and I escaped on our bikes — out to the beach at South Bar to pick gallons of blueberries to sell to each others' mothers when they got together to play tarbish on Saturday nights. When I was seven, I got picked up by the cops for thumbing a ride on the Overpass into the city. That was the first time Ma made me promise never to hitchhike again.

"You little beatnik," she teased me as I dried her tears and kissed her.

"What's a beatnik?" I asked, but she wouldn't say.

Three days after Darla's goodbye, I got picked up by the cops hitchhiking across the Causeway to the mainland, Nova Scotia. I'd gotten beyond the Overpass and the city but, not far away enough.

Ma's maiden name was Ruffman. Years later, when I transitioned from female to male, I took her last name as my first name: Ruf. Half of her last name, anyway. My new last name was inspired by something Pa used to yell at me all the time from his La-Z-Boy in front of the TV: "Grow up and face the real world, kid. Whadda ya think it's gonna be like? Paradise?"

The Adventures of Menstrual Man!!
She lay there gripped with the most painful menstrual cramps until...
Don't fear, I can help!!
JASMIN
Herbal tinctures such as motherwort, crampbark, ginger, & peppermint are very effective...

..and an epsom salt bath works miracles.
If the pain continues remember this...
...sending loving relaxed energy to your ueterus has been proven to provide more pain relief than four letter words.
thanks... whoever you are.

Artist's Statement

Menstrual man is a superhero that I made up to save me from the agony that has been my period. Why is Menstrual Man a man and not a woman? When I drew him/her, s/he just ended up looking like a guy, and all of the other characters I drew also thought s/he was a guy. in any event, if you look closely, you'll notice that he's menstruating.

— *Susan Justin*

out of the frying pan

Daphne Gottlieb

All I can tell you is about memory, she's been gone so long, the woman I thought I loved, who I was taught to love, who never existed at all. She was warm ample brown skin, she was nothing of the sort. She was a legend, a woman who fed a batallion of soldiers with just eggs, sugar, and flour. She was soft as water and cloth and sugar, a sugartit; strong, healthy, and resilient as a cast iron pan. She was none of this. She's just a red bandanna on an actress. She was just another sale on bodies already stolen. She's a cardboard image held down by shackles. When I see Uncle Sam's plantation now, from a distance, her cardboard image is on fire, but never ashes, never burned. There are shackles on the ground where she was, right above the "Hearn Texas Chamber of Commerce" plaque. In the distance, you can see an advertising executive, rolled in Quaker Oats, running into the swamp. There's an unfinished dress made of curtains on the ground. There's nothing else except sour milk that smells like tar. I know exactly how to measure where her body is missing from how wide to hold my arms. I know to name everything that's missing; it's the same name she always had. Jemima.

in the beginning, there was algoma

Dani Couture

named after the steel mill
where her father toiled, al was born
with curved ribs of rusting rebar,
a white-hot coke oven for a mouth –
a mouth that would just as easily consume
you, as talk to you. in the beginning,

there were crisp fields of wildflowers;
al was named after these, too.
this was before the factory,
before big box, before black metal
basement bands – before a city on the brink
of becoming a town, then nothing.
algoma dreamed flat on her back.
two months of summer
never enough to melt ten months of snow.

the third shift is already going in,
and she is not even awake.

Algoma is an Ojibwa word that means "Valley of Flowers."

algoma looks at the stars

Dani Couture

through her own skin; two binary freckles
at her left elbow, a dense constellation
across the razor thin bridge of her nose,
and a red supernova caught mid-
explosion within the thin skin of her back.
only she is aware of her pale flesh map —
this one charted piece of night sky.
she knows where every star belongs, has named each
according to its brilliance, distance, and arrangement.
listen to the velocity of her words.
she is white hot with the world she holds without her hands.

How to Become a Rodeo Queen

Michelle Mach

1. The Queen is an ambassador of the American West Rodeo, Inc. It is her duty and obligation to portray the highest moral standards and showcase the ideals of womanhood.

Ideals? Breanna? Oh, please. When the judges asked about her greatest ambitions during tryouts, she looked puzzled and said, "Emissions? Like gas?" How she got elected Queen instead of me, I'll never know.

2. It is the Queen's responsibility to keep herself neat, clean, and well-groomed at all times. If your hat comes off while at the rodeo, your head better be in it.

Standing behind a tree, I watched a flushed and rumpled Breanna step out of a cowboy's trailer.

Matchmaking magic! I ran ahead to our trailer, almost knocking over our chaperone, Ms. Fitz. When Breanna finally strolled in, Ms. Fitz delivered a finger-shaking, tongue-clucking lecture. "Other queens have lost their crowns for less." Breanna just shrugged and turned to me. "Did you finish starching my jeans, Amy? And what about my boots? Polished yet?"

3. The Queen agrees to attend every rodeo within 350 miles of headquarters. Attendance at additional parades, festivals, and fairs may also be required.

I had no idea where I was. Somewhere in Oregon, perhaps. While Breanna napped, I explored some fields far from the screams and squeaks of the carnival rides. I tossed a bouquet of black locust leaves and foxglove and curtseyed to an imaginary audience. Later, I fixed Breanna a salad with my handpicked treasures, artfully arranging each leaf. "No thanks," she said, waving it away. Fine! I stomped over to the stable and delivered my masterpiece to a more appreciative audience.

4. The Queen is responsible for having her horse, pickup, and trailer ready at all times. The horse should be shod, fit, groomed, and ready to ride.

Breanna has a beautiful quarter horse named Sunshine that she's been riding since she was twelve. The vet said that Sunshine's partial paralysis was probably from something she ate. Nothing permanent, but now I hurried to apply hoof polish to the replacement horse. Breanna fluffed the new horse's tail. That whole big hair dream doesn't stop with humans. I dropped the rag I was using and the horse skittered. I stroked its mane to soothe it. "Come on, Amy," said Breanna. "Almost showtime."

An hour later, I sat with Ms. Fitz and watched Breanna shoot out of the gate like a pinball. The air smelled like always, of horse manure and cotton candy. Just as Breanna rounded the corner, my program accidentally fluttered into the ring. The horse reared, its legs climbing air.

5. In the event that the Queen cannot complete her reign, the runner-up should be prepared to take her place.

Breanna fell. For a moment, everything stood still except for clouds of dust. Then a scramble of clowns and paramedics. The rodeo board looked worried, so I stood up and gave a perfect Queen's wave. Good thing I don't quit easy.

I See Now That Brown Owl Was a Lesbian

Bren Simmers

Rumour had it she was a dropout from consciousness-raising groups, having traded in her jeans and plaid shirt for another uniform: brown dress, sash, and camp hat. I know now it was the whistle she liked best, not having to wait her turn through endless meetings in somebody else's living room. That shrill whistle silenced the chatter. Even the most unruly girls, the ones who came for the free hot chocolate and nothing else, fell silent.

Brown Owl disagreed with Audre Lorde about the master's tools. She preferred to work from within. I imagine a well-thumbed copy of Sappho rubbing up against the Brownie motto in her leather pouch. She'd never threaded a needle in her life and here she was teaching us crafts and Christian folk songs. *Kumbaya, my lord, kumbaya,* her voice low, off-key. Assuring our suburban mothers we would grow up right, always cross our legs in public, remember to say please. As for the girls who shared sleeping bags on camping trips, and those eager to master rope tricks, hog-tying, and lassoing other Brownies during stampede week, Brown Owl kept quiet.

Leprechaun, Fairy, Sprite, Pixie, or Elf, when it came time for us to split up into groups, one in each corner of the church basement, almost every girl wanted to be a Fairy, soft-spoken, light on her feet. Brown Owl didn't have the heart to tell us that what we were destined to be was *girls,* guided through the rituals of matching knee socks, hosting bottle drives, and selling those damn cookies. Lined up, she counted us off one to ten. No one understood her complicated math, but we squirmed and pinched for a better position. A one meant you got to be a Fairy.

The Madwoman

Rose Cullis

When I was fourteen, I decided that going mad was a kind of optional occupation, and that it had a lot of attendant privileges that were worth considering. I welcomed the idea of prolonged hospital stays with very little expected of me, the concerned attention of doctors in uniform and well-pressed nurses, the little pills in paper cups administered several times daily, and the dramatic encounters with orderlies that ended in enforced sedation. I decided that going mad could be a very engaging activity, and that it provided a forum for a kind of obscure performance art that would be at once purging, heartfelt, and vengeful. Going mad was something I could be really, really good at, and I set out at once to accomplish it.

It wasn't hard to begin. There were a number of precedents that made "coming out," so to speak, easier. My older sister had already achieved some status by becoming unhinged in the principal's office at school. She'd forged my father's signature on a note, and when the nasty vice principal – who had a penchant for kneeling in front of girls in miniskirts, to take a measure of the distance between their hems and their knees – became suspicious about the typed note and called my father, my sister did something so big, so loud, so terrifying, that they called an ambulance instead. This event sent shock waves through the family. My parents began convening family meetings at the doomed dinner table, and tried on their own awkward version of group therapy. They groveled and lied about their intentions with respect to my younger sister and me, and even tried to hug us for a while. It was horrible, but it was impressive and theatrical and satisfying.

In Scarborough in the seventies, it was "in" to be crazy. I knew other kids would be jealous of me, if I managed to pull it off. My mother liked to claim that it was just my crowd that had these sick obsessions with sickness, but in fact – except for a few losers, who didn't get it – going mad was highly respectable. It was renowned as an artist's exploit, for one thing. All artists were mad. We all knew that. And we hadn't questioned the logic of inverting the statement, and concluding that all mad people were necessarily artists. There was even a kind of fashion statement in place. Kids OD'd for hospital bracelets and boasted of their exploits later. The best thing was to be admitted to the psych ward on the tenth floor of the local hospital – we called it Tower Ten – and escape. To push open the buzzing exit door and rush down the ten flights with your heart pounding, where your old friend C.B. waited outside next to her Datsun, holding the door open. Or better still: to make your way to the local highway, with your hospital robe snapping in the wind, and attempt to thumb a ride home, only to be picked up in an ambulance and hustled back for another rousing adventure.

Tower Ten. Even the name appealed to me.

Sometimes I try to work out when my obsession with "the madwoman" began. I remember sitting on the tile floor in the living room of my parents' bungalow, when I was a small child, watching Audrey Hepburn encounter a madwoman in a film entitled *The Nun's Story*. I was wearing a short, frothy dress because I was a girl, and my mother had cropped my hair into a pixie-cut because it was easy to take care of. I had jewel-blue horn-rimmed glasses in those days, and my father insisted that all of his daughters wear black Oxfords. At six, then, I was Elvis Costello – sitting with my scratchy crinoline arranged around me, periodically peeling my thighs from the linoleum, while I watched Audrey make her way down a dark corridor of cells in her sweet little black and white nun's habit, carrying a tray of tin cups.

Audrey looks good. Her hair has been cropped off in an earlier scene, in some kind of ecstatic denial of womanly pride, and her short dark bangs look waifish and stylish. She's trembling. Tentative. Each cell she passes has a tiny little window with rusted bars, and she can see hands and fingers poking plaintively out of them. Audrey tries to pay no attention to the owners of the hands. She tries not to be seduced by the sounds and sights of madness reaching for her – by the whining and the whimpering and the whispering. One woman rasps, "Give me a drink! My throat is parched," and Audrey is forced to look. The imprisoned woman has clearly been there a long time. She's of some indeterminate age. Her long hair is in matted ropes, and her eyes glitter. "My throat is parched," she whimpers. "Have mercy." Now Audrey Hepburn knows just how devious and desperate madwomen are. Nonetheless – and just in case God is watching – Audrey feels forced to exercise a little Christian compassion. She takes a tin cup in her long, slender, implausibly-manicured fingers, and passes it to the woman. The woman grabs Audrey's wrist and reaches for her throat. Audrey screams and the woman laughs, a strange and peculiar kind of laugh, focused and deliberate, empty and taunting. A mad laugh.

"They're coming to take me away, ha ha."

Once – when I was very little – I saw a mad*man* on TV. The madman was some kind of psychotic killer, of course, and he had a strange grin. Before he killed someone, he'd turn to the camera and grin. I turned away from the TV in horror. I was four or five years old, and this smiling man with his glazed eyes and his sadistic intent terrified me. I turned away to find my father behind me, grinning like the madman on TV, and committed to delighting me further with more escapades in sheer terror.

Time to play with the children. My mother stood nearby, looking all sweet and vague and sympathetic. No help there.

So it's difficult to say when I stopped running away from the image of the madwoman and began instead to run directly toward her, with the explicit intention of becoming her, in all her messy, confrontational bloody-mindedness.

At fourteen, I find myself charmed by strange little vignettes. I picture myself – sullen and full-lipped, with dark brooding eyes and an impossibly slender body wrapped in a terrycloth housecoat – sitting in a TV room in the psych ward, flicking ashes from my cigarette, too sensitive to participate in regular conversations. I picture men seeing me like this, and being moved to a terrible and tender desire for me that is doomed to remain unrequited because I am really quite, quite mad. I imagine people — nurses, doctors — discussing my case. Fretting over the particulars: the rage-crazed father, the tender, timid mother. "How is she?" "Not very well." — whispered in the next room — while I/me, the mad poet, am the product of, pressed into shape by, the intensity of a family history which I am not responsible for, or reducible to — to which I bring only my helpless, trembling, musical box of a body. My instrument. Me.

As a result, and after some consideration, I settle on OD'ing as the easiest and most obvious means of ensuring that I will make it to Tower Ten, for my first real performance.

It wasn't as easy as I expected it to be. It wasn't as easy to "make it stick," anyway. One day — one January morning — I took an overdose of some over-the-counter pill. I had no intention of dying, and no way of knowing if what I'd consumed was sufficient, but it did strike me as sufficiently dramatic for my purposes. I took the pills carefully and deliberately, and then wondered what to do next. Class had already started, so one possibility was to stumble to school and alert the audience there. But by then, it might be too late. It definitely seemed a little anti-climactic to call an ambulance myself. Accordingly, I put my peajacket on and headed down the street to seek some hapless neighbour who might serve me as an accomplice.

It was a dark and dirty day. No one else was out and about. It was the suburbs, after all, so walking was rarely employed as a means of getting somewhere. I walked, anyway, down the empty street — past the houses with their grinning front doors, their gleaming windows, their jutting garages. Most of them had aluminum siding on the second floor, and the effect — so it seemed to me in the state of feverish lateral thinking that I was practicing at the time — was to make them look like implacable, unshaven faces.

Then I got lucky. At the bottom of the street, I saw a man cleaning off his car. He was a middle-aged man, nervous and obedient-looking. I staggered up to my chosen one and told him that I'd just taken an overdose, and I needed to be taken to a doctor right away. I suppressed a sob, and trembled. I barely remember his reaction, but he drove me to a clinic.

I sat on the floor of the clinic, slumped against an empty chair, examining my hands, as if there was something quite fascinating there. I was soon ushered on a stretcher to a white room where pharmaceutical samples were laid out on the counter. My senses were on fire. I sat up on the stretcher for a while, before the whole thing struck me as woefully inadequate for my purposes. I rose and went over to the corner and pressed myself into it, rubbing my cheeks against the white walls, covering my head with my arms. I slumped down to the floor and wept. I made my agony a thing of beauty.

Just in time, the doctor appeared. He asked me what I had taken. I considered evading the question, but realized that I was a little too conscious to pull that one off, so I confessed, and my heart dropped at the look of relief on his face. Time to turn up the heat. I traced the walls with my fingers, tears running down my cheeks. I began mumbling incoherently, as if the drugs were taking effect — although I actually felt nothing. He left the room, and came back uttering the words I wanted to hear.

I've called an ambulance. They'll be here soon.

An ambulance! In no time at all, I was sitting up on another stretcher in the emergency ward of the local hospital waiting to have my stomach pumped. At least that's what I was hoping for. The phrase itself pleased me. I imagined myself telling my friends later, "I had to get my stomach pumped." Instead, they fed me some sort of mustardy potion, and then encouraged me to drink lots of ginger ale. The idea was that I would participate in this purging by drinking ginger ale till I vomited up the contents of my stomach. I did it, although I wasn't pleased — and midway through, my sweet mother entered the room in an uncommon temper. She hustled over to the bed where ginger ale dripped from my nose.

"This is the last time you'll be up to this, young lady," she said.

I was amazed that she might infer that I'd undertaken this whole event consciously. What kind of mother thinks that a teenager might derive pleasure from OD'ing and landing in a hospital? Even if it's true — what kind of mother comprehends these things, and responds to a suicide attempt with this unloving comment? I couldn't blame the doctors. They had, apparently, recommended that I stay for a while. They told her that I'd just be back. But my mother knew better. It was one thing for a man to indulge himself with outbursts that were so passionate that they verged on erotic. A young girl had other responsibilities. A young girl was supposed to be caring and empathetic — not monstrously self-absorbed and histrionic. If my mother could have, she would have grabbed me by the hair and dragged me out of there — she was so aggravated by the whole display.

The doctors were right, of course — in the sense that I would be back. My mother's tight-lipped disapproval was hardly enough to interrupt the grip the madwoman had on my imagination, and the fierce way I identified with it. I was disappointed that my first efforts were not as fruitful as my sister's breakdown had been, but I resolved to study it further.

What I remember best about her are the corndogs her mother brought to the hospital to tempt her with. She'd be sitting on the couch, resplendent in her shabby housecoat, looking pouty and despondent, her head turned away from the proffered corndog while I watched — from behind curtains, it seems in my memory — like some kind of doomed Polonius.

I'd never seen corndogs before. It seems incredible. I was, after all, a suburban girl. But I was also sheltered. Isolated, even. When I was younger, all the kids in my class seemed to go bowling on Saturday mornings, for example. And it seemed like their parents went with them. They *all* went bowling on Saturdays — and they probably ate corndogs and drank Coca Cola then, too — while I woke up and played Barbies with my sister under the table in the basement laundry room where we kept our collection of toys. Our makeshift toy room. Our safe room.

My family had managed to fashion a kind of craggy, *Wuthering Heights* existence inside the four-bedroom, two-storey house that my parents had picked from the models offered by the builders. It was there that I first learned my craft — witnessed the bulging eyes, the words muttered through ground teeth, and the peculiar pitch of voice that signals the existence of some kind of terrible pressure that wants out. My father chased me up the stairway once, with a scream so high-pitched that only the whimpering dog could hear it. My older sister climbed into my bed at night, made a tent out of the sheets, and told me lurid tales. "They cut a hole in your leg," she told me once. "Then they stick it in."

"Doesn't it bleed?" I couldn't help but discern the pleasure she took in sharing her horror with me, but I was too stupid to keep my mouth shut to avoid further revelations. "Doesn't it bleed?"

"Everywhere!" she promised.

So I knew what high drama looked like; my body sympathetically resonated with the shape of it. I had only to touch it a little more deliberately, to sound it out.

The corndogs looked delicious. I was absolutely charmed by the crafty way the hot dog had been embedded in the cornbread. When I felt my mouth watering, and even felt pity for the mother, I knew that this girl was my superior in the labour of loud lamenting. There her pitiful mother was: crooning with concern, leaning forward with one arm extended, and reaching for a strand of the corndog girl's fallen hair. There I was: watching, wondering, hungry.

I turned away and one of the social workers grabbed my elbow. He was a youngish, hip kind of guy — the sort of guy who modelled himself on Jack Kerouac — and I aggravated him. He would have loved it if I were several years older and eager to give him a blowjob at a party, but my current lower-middle-class Ophelia-thing was just too much. He dragged me into a small closet, and decided to set the record straight.

"I know what you're doing," he said, "with your 'poor little Goldilocks' routine. You might be taking Taylor for a ride, but I know what you're doing. I know it's all intentional, and that it's just a big act."

Taylor was *my* social worker, and *he* was a big romantic of sorts, in the sense that he had no idea what I was doing, and was desperate to help me. He'd sit with me with a sad, sympathetic expression on his gentle face and try to teach me about the theories that were in vogue at the time. He'd tell me that anger was depression and depression was anger turned inwards, and he'd try to explain the worst thing I could do to someone.

"Do you know what it is?"

"No." I was barely listening, but turned respectfully toward him, because he was such a nice guy. My eyes were turned in, and pondering my next action.

"To accuse someone of 'not caring'."

What? I stopped contriving for a snap second, because I was so surprised at the pathetic banality of his reasoning. What if someone really didn't care? Was it still "the worst thing"? Why was he telling me this? It didn't strike me as a fundamental feature of my malingering.

Still, I liked Taylor — way more than I liked his lascivious and astute compatriot in social work. I admired Taylor's commitment to helping me, even though he really had no idea what was going on. I tried to please him, at times, by faking a kind of recovery, but it was way, way too late. The show had begun.

I'd made it to Tower Ten. I'd even felt delight at the sight of my special bed in the dorm room of the disaffected — with its white sheets pulled tight, and the promise of metalwork gleaming under the frame. But soon, it became too obvious that my status on the ward was minimal. When the nurses arrived with their cups and their pills and their large popsicle sticks and dispensers for efficient counting, I was either ignored altogether, or handed a very minor yellow valium at bedtime. Yellow! Five milligrams! I was ashamed that this was my allotment, and jealously eyed what the others got. Once, I even managed to steal a small cup of very large tablets. I took them instantly, and within an hour the world was flattened, colours were muted, my limbs were under water, and my tongue was swollen and useless. That was a serious drug.

The corndog girl knew how to be taken seriously. She knew how to command an audience – how to make them rapt. Once, in a raucous altercation with her panting mother, she ran screaming into one of the bathrooms and smashed something against the sink. She grabbed a piece of the cracked porcelain and started hacking at herself with it. The entire ward was abuzz with the emergency. Lights strobed. Her mother wailed. Nurses careened down the halls with stretchers and other accessories. The orderlies struggled to hold her down. I was sent (not even dragged!) away – like the minor player I was.

I realized then that more was expected of me. I couldn't simply swallow an indeterminate amount of pills and weep into walls. I had to be willing to lay the integrity of the very margins of my self – of my tender skin – on the line. I had to literally split myself open in order to spill out whole and new.

I can't tell you how satisfying it is to find a surefire means of horrifying people. Even today – with my arms still scarred with burn and bite marks, and with various Frankenstein-like slashes cross-hatched with stitches – I look back, and feel a certain pride in the ends I was willing to go to. At the time, the sheer ease of the performance surprised me. I thought it would be difficult. I thought the pain might make me pause. But instead, the pain was a kind of purgative. Post-self-abuse, I always felt a wash of deep relaxation. The deed was done. The hieroglyphs were carved and posted for public viewing.

I particularly loved getting sewn up. The tut-tut of the focused doctor. The fresh white winding cloths. Again, I had no intention of bleeding to death. I even had some confidence that this was physically impossible. My older sister had grabbed me in the bathroom once, and held me in a backwards embrace, tracing her finger along my throat.

"If you really want to kill yourself," she said, calling my bluff, "you have to cut the jugular vein. Here."

I still hadn't quite cracked the psych ward, though. They kept bringing me in and releasing me soon after — as an out-patient. One day, I decided that I'd had quite enough of this dilly-dallying, that it was time to affect a "break-in" so to speak. I put some caps of MDA in one pocket, and a brand new razor-blade in the other — as a kind of back-up plan. I put on my best hip-hugging Lee's cords (sewn up the crotch and around the knees for extra tightness and flare), and my little boy's running shoes, and I outlined my big blue eyes in black kohl.

At school, I took all the MDA, and reported to the school nurse that I'd taken an overdose. She called an ambulance and I was taken to the hospital. By now, this was all routine, and barely registered for me as a real "scene." I got to the hospital — mission #1 accomplished — and skulked around the halls, listening for their intentions with respect to my fate. Sure enough, they were planning to discharge me that afternoon. *I don't think so,* I thought, and my confidence felt good. I felt like I finally had some control over the situation. I knew how to proceed next — to ensure that I achieved what I wanted.

I went into one of the washrooms. I took the razor out of my back pocket, and slowly, deliberately, slashed my wrists — making sure that it was deep enough that the skin gaped open and necessitated stitches. Satisfied that the wounds were sufficient, I lay back on the terrazzo floor with my arms extended in an intentional invocation of Christ's suffering on the cross. The blood slipped down my hands and stained the floors. I waited, patiently. After a while, I heard them outside. In my mind's eye, they were even enquiring about my whereabouts with some concern. Her? Her? Where is she? Here, behind the steel door in bright technicolour, wondering when you'll finally look. Someone looked. She screamed and the heavy door shut temporarily. I heard a skirmishing outside, and permitted myself a small secret smile.

Soon I was careening down the hall on a stretcher. It was my ultimate saviour fantasy, made even sweeter by the tourniquets on my arms ("Surely I don't need that," I said demurely), and the panting nurses at my side. Under bright hot lights, they sewed me up and stripped me down — and strapped me to a bed in the observation room.

And there I lay — restrained and satisfied, weary and proud. I'd achieved my goals. I was a madwoman: firmly, clinically insane, and clearly considered dangerous.

Percy, 1980

Suzy Malik & Zoe Whittall

SWIMMING OUT FROM MY SPINE ARE WINGS FASHIONED FROM FISHING WIRE. THEY DO NOT ITCH WHEN FASTENED PROPERLY.

I SAVE.
I AM A COLLECTOR OF ILL WILL. I TAKE IT IN AND LET IT GO. BREATHING IS EASY WHEN IT'S SLOW ENOUGH.

TIGHT LIPS.

WHERE DOES YOUR HEART DROP, WHEN IT GETS HARD AND FALLS?

IF YOU WERE A MIRACLE, WHAT WOULD YOU BE?

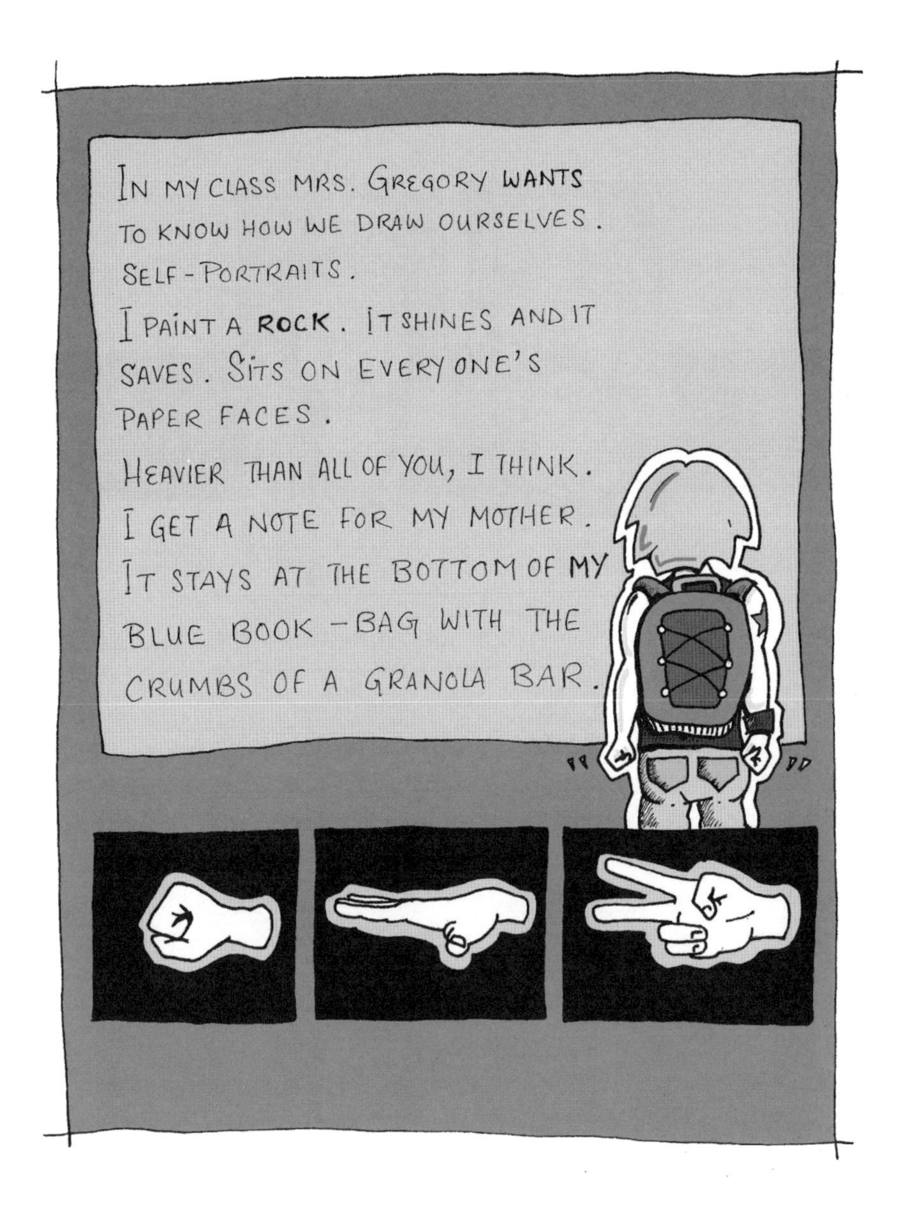
IN MY CLASS MRS. GREGORY WANTS
TO KNOW HOW WE DRAW OURSELVES.
SELF-PORTRAITS.
I PAINT A ROCK. IT SHINES AND IT
SAVES. SITS ON EVERYONE'S
PAPER FACES.
HEAVIER THAN ALL OF YOU, I THINK.
I GET A NOTE FOR MY MOTHER.
IT STAYS AT THE BOTTOM OF MY
BLUE BOOK-BAG WITH THE
CRUMBS OF A GRANOLA BAR.

IZABELLE DRAWS A STICK FIGURE WITH SMALL ARMS. THE BIGGEST THING **ON** THE EXPANSIVE PIECE OF INDUSTRIAL YELLOWED PAPER ARE HER EYES.

"WHY ARE YOUR EYES SO **BIG?**"

ASKS MRS. GREGORY.

SHE SHRUGS. BEAUTIFULLY. LATER, ON THE BUS, SHE PULLS OUT THE DRAWING. "MY EYES ARE BIG BECAUSE WHEN I SEE TOO MUCH THEY GET **SORE**. EVEN WHEN I CLOSE MY EYES, I STILL SEE." SHE RIPS THE PAPER INTO TINY MOLECULES. THE STARS OF WINTER TRAILING WITH THE YELLOW BUS EXHAUST.

I TRY TO HOLD HER HAND. SHE PINCHES ME ...
EXIT
"YOU'RE WEIRD."

TUESDAYS NOW, WHEN THE REST OF THE CLASS GOES TO THE POOL FOR SWIM LESSONS, I SIT WITH MR. BROSSARD TO TALK ABOUT MY PROBLEMS.
I DON'T HAVE PROBLEMS I THINK.
I HAVE WISHES.
I HAVE VISIONS.
I HAVE AN ENDLESS ABILITY TO HEAL.

I GIVE HER A SHINY PINK BAND-AID ON FRIDAY WHEN SHE SKATES INTO THE ICE WITH HER RIGHT KNEE. SHE DOESN'T SAY THANK-YOU BUT SHE SMILES. SHE THROWS HER SKATES OVER HER SHOULDER AND DOESN'T HAVE GUARDS ON THEM.

THEY SAY, THE NEXT DAY, THAT SHE WOULD HAVE FROZEN INTO SLEEP. NO SHOES IN THE SNOW BANK BY HIGHWAY FIVE.

I WAS A HERO.

I GET MY PHOTO ON PAGE 2 OF THE GRAVY RIVER WEEKLY.

I KNOW NOW, WHEN TO SHUT UP. I DO NOT SAY I DREAMT HER. AN ANGEL ALONE WITHOUT SHOES ON THE SIDE OF THE HIGHWAY. I WALKED TO HER WHEN I WOKE UP, 5 AM, CARRYING A PAIR OF BOOTS & A BLANKET.

NO QUESTIONING JUST FOOT BY FOOT FORWARD.

SHE LOOKED STILL. QUIET. AN ICICLE.

LIKE THE DREAM SAID IN THICK BLOCK LETTERS . . . **GO**

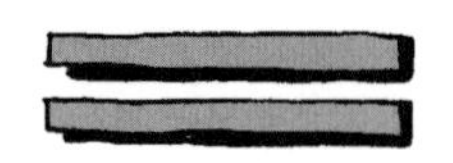

"YOU'RE BARELY 50 POUNDS LITTLE ONE, THERE'S NO WAY
YOU CARRIED HER ALL THAT WAY BY YOURSELF!" "ADRENALINE"
MY MOTHER SUGGESTS "LIKE WHEN PEOPLE LIFT CARS BY
THEMSELVES TO SAVE OTHERS." I KNEW IT WAS MORE THAN
THAT. BUT I HELD MY TONGUE. A SECRET. FLATTEN MY
WIRED WINGS INTO MY BACK SO THAT THEY'RE AN
OUTLINE HIDDEN, UNLESS YOU LOOK CLOSELY WITH
BIG EYES.

The Avon Lady

Bren Simmers

Lou Ann was our Avon Lady, a brunette with a do-it-yourself dye job, small blue eyes rimmed in black pencil. Her skin was carefully blended to the hairline, a medium beige. Thursday nights, she came calling. Our matching cups and saucers sat on the table as we waited for her entrance — a flourish of bangles and miracle creams.

She could talk the ear off a horse, my mother said, but at least she could carry on a conversation, which was more than she could say for the neighbourhood ladies around here. What I liked about her was that she knew where our spoons were kept and thanks hon, but if she needed more sugar she could get it herself.

Her fingers thick with rings as she spread the latest merchandise out before my mother, paused dramatically, then began. Building the foundation, curling the lashes, Lou Ann's eyes taking in every pore. Suck in your cheeks, she'd say, stroking blush along bone. You really ought to play up your lips. Or lift your chin a moment — there. Lou Ann holding a mirror up to my mother's newly polished face, while I sat hopeful in the chair beside her. My best smile on, the one I saved for relatives. I longed for the hint of shimmer to gloss my lips, for samples to line up in the bathroom like boys to be kissed. For Lou Ann to powder my T-Zone, outline my lips in Cherry Pout. Transformed, I could join in. Cross my legs, uncross. One cream or two.

But they always talked about people I didn't know and sooner or later my mother would ask me to go get her purse from upstairs, signaling the end of the visit. With a sweep of Lou Ann's arms, the array of products would disappear and a single compact or tube would be all that was left. The magic of it: no matter how much my mother bought, there was always more, waiting in the hidden pockets and zippers of that leather handbag.

Between her visits, we sat around a dog-eared catalogue, pens in hand, adding and subtracting prices in the margins. My mother's face . . . Imari, Skin So Soft, Anew.

Betty

Bren Simmers

I was eight when I won her Easy-Bake oven, complete with cake mixes, light bulb, and red apron. Until then I was a beater of eggs, a licker of spoons, a taster of batters. Now I was a protégé, a medium through which Betty Crocker could channel her secret recipes: Cookies 'n' Cream, Chocolate Turtle Surprise, Magician's Bunny Cake.

Supervision required, the instructions said, but that didn't stop me. I had work to do. My mother braced herself for the worst, but trouble didn't start until I ran out of cake mixes. Betty never told me what was in them. Staring at the kitchen cupboards, I waited for inspiration, some kind of sign, until Betty's voice whispered in my ear: *something wet and something dry.* That was it! Cocoa powder and sugar, vanilla and milk. Betty making promises of *super-moist, rich and creamy.*

I didn't believe my mother when she told me that my teeth would rot, that nothing good comes from a box, or that Crocker was two eggs short of a dozen. I was confident that with a little help from Betty, anything we made would turn out right. When my teddy bear lost his arm in a tug-of-war, I was convinced I could bake it back on. I placed him gingerly inside the oven, arm snug against body for a perfect fit, and cranked the dial to 400°. Betty and I peered through the tinted glass together, the timer ticking out its magic.

57 saviours, or palms up

Dani Couture

told she would
die
at birth, again
at 24, and
the latest estimate, 43,
my mother collects
yard sale saviours. 25 cent
salvation is not only cheap,
but transferable.
others are so eager
to cell ceramic
madonnas and plastic
jesuses. hand-made.
some have been
glued
back together and
touched
up with nail polish.
mary's lips are foiled
flirtation red.

in my mother's bedroom,
each saviour,
man or woman,
stands
on its own
halo:
a crisp doily, also
hand-made.
they are all waiting
for an opportunity
to save.
and no one points out
how my mother's
porcelain army
outnumbers her years
and the time
she has
spent waiting
out death,
a handful
of change
at a time.

Barbie Double-Dates (confessions of an eighties child)

Allison Moore

There isn't much room in my life for multiple worships. My parents forbid me from sticking things onto the wall, and with my growing collection of slinkies, there is only one shelf left on my bookcase. Not much room for objects of worship. I should ask my parents about expanding my furniture options but alas, I am ten years old, remembering to brush my teeth is task enough. So I have a decision to make. The top shelf is the priority shelf and I've made the momentous decision to push the slinkies aside as someone is moving in — either Barbie or Madonna. It's a tough decision. Madonna has been in my life for a while, but Barbie, well . . . she is quickly becoming an important part of my sexual development.

It's the weekend and my friend Lana is over. We are sitting in the basement. Every now and again, in heavy rain, it floods down here so my parents have ripped up the carpet. On the bare concrete, I have drawn chalked outlines of little squares joined by invisible force — a floor plan. I saw this quite clearly as I drew the plan; my imagination holds all the secrets. Lana sees the scribbles. She asks me what they are and I shrug my shoulders. I don't want to tell her this is Barbie's house. She has the horse and the car and the caravan, and I have chalk on concrete.

Lana and I have recently decided to be best friends. It was a momentous occasion which involved much conversation and even more letter writing. We have decided this based on two important criteria. Firstly, we live across the road from each other. Secondly, Lana has an excellent Barbie collection.

Lana brings all the Barbie accessories to our rendezvous in the basement, and she also brings Ken. He doesn't come with any great enthusiasm;

he is thrown in with all the other stuff in her Barbie Box. Ken's role in our Barbie playing is questionable at best. He is only ever a supporting character, and is often left sitting on a chair, lying on a bed, or simply thrown across the floor while our two Barbies engage in long exciting adventures.

Ken is boring. He is always naked (Lana lost his clothes some time ago) and he offers nothing to the imagination of two ten-year-old girls. How can we relate to this naked, bronzed muscle man/doll? So while it might be imagined that Ken and Barbie would relate to each other sexually, this was never the case. If they did happen to find themselves in bed, they were always there to sleep. Lana and I had no desire to sexualize our Barbies; we were too busy doing that to each other.

We are sitting in my parents' hot tub. Our Barbies sit beside us, in their own. Lana's hot tub, as she reminds me a little too often. We had played with our Barbies for a while, but they are getting the silent treatment now. We are kissing. We know this is something that we shouldn't allow our parents to see. We don't know it is wrong necessarily, but we don't think it is right either.

We pull the hot tub cover over our heads and our Barbies fall to the ground, but we don't notice. We explore each other's bodies silently. I am three months older than her and I feel great responsibility with this difference in age. I don't want her to be uncomfortable. I also do not want her to tell on me. The sense of wrongdoing is growing with every inch of body I am exploring. Our ears are pricked. We don't want to be caught.

My mother yells for me and we quickly adjust our swim suits to their correct positions. My mother arrives at the back door just as we resume playing with our Barbies. We must look cute; two little girls playing with their Barbies in the little Barbie hot tub.

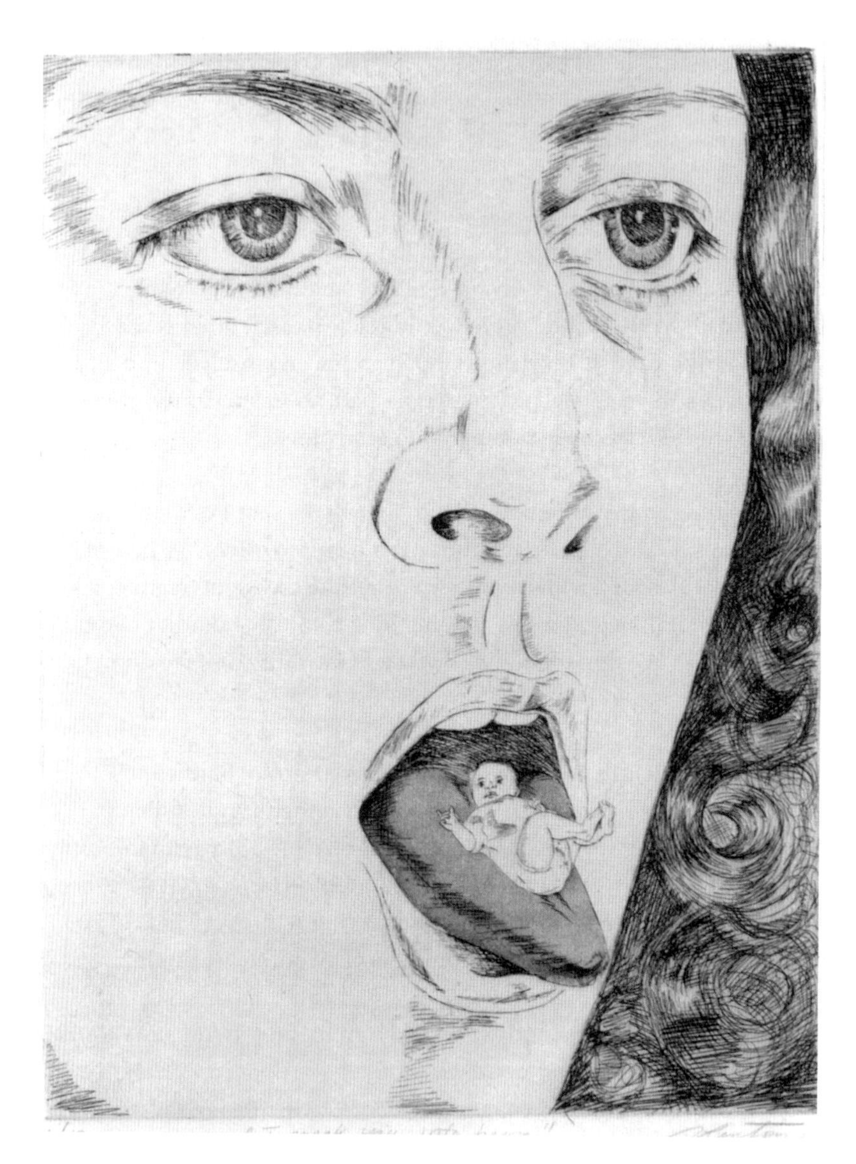

I Speak You Into Being, Jennifer Linton

The Rapture, Jennifer Linton

Judith, Jennifer Linton

Artist's Statement

The Rapture and *Judith* belong to a body of work entitled "St. Ursula & the Eleven Thousand Virgins." In these autobiographically inspired drawings and etchings, I have borrowed the identity of St. Ursula, the patron saint of school girls, and transformed her into a guardian angel/sword-wielding avenger for the purposes of exploring themes of child abuse, female sexuality, and the idea of virginity. My vision of St. Ursula is one of a protector and guide for prepubescent girls who face a world that is exploitative of their bodies and sexualities. *Judith* is an ancient Jewish heroine who beheads the Assyrian general Holofernes who is waging war against her people. *The Rapture* is an imagined, psychosexual, quasi-religious vision (think "Ecstasy of St. Teresa," but with a sword).

I Speak You Into Being belongs to a new body of work entitled "Gravid," which addresses the theme of motherhood. It's an ambivalent image that hints at various creation myths (gods literally "speaking" humanity into existence), while simultaneously suggesting stories such as Cronos (Saturn) devouring his children, or, for that matter, the Eucharist. This series more broadly speaks to societal notions of motherhood, both through stereotypes of the "good" and "bad" mother.

– *Jennifer Linton*

Lipstick Boys

Sandra Alland

It was a time of rubber bracelets
and non-symmetrical hair.
We were all off-kilter growing,
some parts faster than others.

I learned masturbation tactics
from songs:
Cyndi she-bopping and
Madonna getting into the groove.
Magical femme words
that guided my hands
to lock doors
and find deep parts of me
that, at ten,
I had already taken for dead.

I was obsessed with Boy George,
confused by his name because
he was my favourite girl of all.
I wanted long braids
and flowing multicoloured outfits,
imagined myself on trial
like in the video, begging:

Do you really want to make me cry?

Diva fantasies, yet
oddly associated
with loss of power.
Annie Lennox was a force,

but my hero-girl
was disadvantaged,
suffering.

I didn't understand
why,
just knew
I wanted her to make it
so I too could survive.

And we did,
lipstick only slightly smeared.

My Mother, Belle Starr

Roxanne Dunbar Ortiz

I am Pearl Starr, the only daughter of the late Belle Starr, and no one knows the facts about her as I do. My mother was born Myra Belle Shirley. Starr was her second husband's name. Her first husband, my father, was Jim Reed.

The main thing that needs to be known about my mother is that she was a natural-born rebel against injustice, against law enforcers who did the dirty work of the rich, against women being squeezed out of everything important and valuable in life.

There is only one book about my mother, *Bella Starr or the Bandit Queen or the Female Jesse James*, and it has never been out of print since it came out in 1889, just after she was murdered. It is a stupid book full of lies, but because it is the only book on Belle, everyone takes it for gospel. For instance, the lie that Cole Younger was my real father. Not that Belle, or I, had anything against Cole. He and his brothers were friends of ours. But Cole and Belle met only once before I was born, when she was fifteen, and I was not even born for another four years. True, for a time after my father was killed Belle called me Pearl Younger, but that had nothing to do with Cole Younger. It was because Belle lived with Bruce Younger, a cousin of Cole's, for a few years before marrying Sam Starr when I was eleven. After that, I was called Pearl Starr.

But I was born Pearl Reed. I believe that Belle and my father were really in love. I cannot recall much about him. I was only six years old when a deputy sheriff ambushed Jim Reed and shot him to pieces with Winchester fire outside Paris, Texas, in 1874. He had become a fugitive from the law only a year after I was born. He and Belle were on the run, with me in tow, for five years before he was killed.

I think the problem is that men who wrote about my mother couldn't reconcile all the complexities of her character, especially the idea that she could be an independent woman without being some kind of sex maniac. Every man wants to make you an honest woman, sees himself as a missionary to "save" you. Maybe it has to do with the way men lie to themselves about cheating on their wives, that instead they are involved in some civic duty to straighten out us hellions, Jezebels, and whores. But I think it is more about them being threatened by our freedom. A free woman is an outlaw without breaking any law, and all men are lawmen when it comes to women.

The only thing good about the book on Belle is some of the pictures. There is even one of me when I was twenty-one, taken around 1891. They cut out my two girlfriends who were in the picture, maybe because they did not want to admit that Belle Starr's daughter was a working girl in the sex trade, like I have been my entire adult life.

There is also a picture of our little ramshackle house at Youngers' Bend in the Cherokee Nation. This is where Belle lived when she was killed, the same house where I grew from a girl to a woman. Anyone who has the idea that outlaws are rich does not know one personally. It is a living, but the best part of it is not the money, as Belle always said, it is the company you keep. That is what life is all about, she always told me.

We moved there is 1880 when Belle married Sam Starr. He was a full-blood Cherokee, son of the famous protector of outlaws, Tom Starr. Of course, I was old enough that I remember everything about that time, which is around when my mother became one of the most famous outlaws in history. Belle was a heroine even to the farm women around there. She made the difference between starving and eating for many a farm family — red, white, and black. And they never forgot.

Just as Belle rose to stardom, things began to fall apart in 1882, when Jesse James was murdered. I could sense the change in Belle and Sam, and I dreaded what was to come even though I had no idea what it might be. It came, all right; the next year the feds arrested Belle and Sam and sent them to the penitentiary. This ended my perfect life. After that, I knew I would be a rebel.

While Belle and Sam were in prison, I lived in Kansas with my grandmother Reed. She had recently taken in an orphan girl named Mabel, who became like a sister to me. She had curly yellow hair and looked like an angel fallen from the heavens. I actually began dreading Belle's release, even though I missed her desperately, because I thought Mabel and I would be separated. I should have known better. When Belle and Sam came for me, they invited Mabel to come live with us.

The first two years back in the Cherokee Nation were a happy time. Mabel and I went to school in nearby Briartown, where we were the only white pupils. We rode our horses to and from school; in fact, all of our free time was spent on our horses. Belle broke a young mare for Mabel and I taught her how to ride and do tricks. We were both determined to join the Wild West Show and become as famous as Annie Oakley and Calamity Jane, not to mention Belle Starr. What most people don't know is that Belle's fame came more from her horsemanship than any kind of banditry, but for that she was punished because women weren't supposed to become famous from such things. Belle was dead set against me joining a western show.

"It's too rough a life and you're finished real young," she said.

Belle wanted me to become a famous writer like Mark Twain. I could not see why it was not possible to be both. One thing Belle did convince me of, though, was that marriage and motherhood were traps for a woman who wanted to make anything of herself.

"If you marry, at least marry a rich man with no less than $25,000 in the bank," Belle cautioned.

I would point out that neither my father Jim Reed nor Sam Starr my stepfather were rich men, and Belle would say, "I'm lucky to have a man like Sam, but most men do not treat their wives as equals and partners like he does."

And I knew she was right. Anyway, she became her own person very young, without having to marry anyone first. I knew I had to do the same – become my own person.

Then I fell in love with a boy two years older who wanted to marry me. He was beautiful, being part Creek and part Cherokee, with long sleek black hair and a face from ancient Rome. His family was poor, but that did not matter to me for I was in love. When we went to Belle and told her we wanted to marry, she sent me away to think on it. But it was a trick. While I was gone, she forged a letter from me telling my sweetheart that I had gone away and married a rich white man. He was heartbroken, he told me later, and went ahead and married the Indian girl his family had long before chosen for him. But when I got back home, we were still in love and met secretly, and in the middle of the summer of 1886, I found myself pregnant.

I didn't tell him, though, as by that time my love for him was fading and I knew I did not want to marry him. I did not tell anyone except Mabel. The only thing I could think of doing was to run away, but I didn't.

Times were not good; a summer of drought and dust and a grasshopper plague, then an early winter and blizzards worse than even the oldest could remember. People were sick and starving. Sam turned to robbing, was indicted, and became a fugitive. Belle had to keep him supplied and I helped. Then she found out I was pregnant and insisted I have an operation.

"You either get rid of that baby or give it away, you're not going to keep it. I won't allow it, won't have you ruining your chances at life," she said.

Belle found money somehow and took me to Fort Smith to the doctor, but I was scared and ran away to Grandma Reed's. Soon after that Sam was killed, and Belle was a widow once again with new problems about whether or not she could remain in the Cherokee Nation. She married James July, a kind of adopted son of Sam Starr. He was part Cherokee and part Choctaw, about sixteen years younger than Belle, and only a few years older than me. Belle made him take her name, and he became known as Billy Starr.

But Belle's life did not concern me then. I had my baby, little Mamie, named after my aunt, Mamie Reed. I did not see Belle again until Mamie was sixteen months old. We did not even write each other, both of us being stubborn.

Then a letter came from Belle saying that my beloved brother Eddie had been shot and was dying, that I should come if I wanted to see him before he died but not to bring my baby. Heavy at heart, I left immediately, thinking I'd be back soon, but that was the last time I saw my baby girl.

Eddie was just fine when I got home. He had been winged in a shooting but healed. Belle had just wanted to get me back, and she had succeeded. She tried to get me to sign a paper turning my baby over to an orphanage. I refused, so she forged my signature and sent it off, and the next thing I knew, she told me my baby was gone.

I was eighteen years old. I guess I just accepted Belle's will and stopped fighting her. We went back to our old life and for the next two years, Belle was my best friend and companion. We rode in every horse race and performed in every wild west show in the area.

The year Belle was murdered, 1889, was the year they opened Oklahoma Territory to white settlers, and Indian Territory was not far behind. There were already fewer Indians than whites living in their own nations even before the government dissolved their governments and parceled out pieces of land back to them, opening what was left over to white homesteaders.

Belle never knew or could have imagined how my life turned out, madam of the biggest brothel in Fort Smith, Arkansas. But I'm not ashamed of being an independent woman. Then again, maybe Belle wouldn't have minded so much. She always told me that outlaws were the only true friends. I'll tell you, it was whores and anarchists who saved my life and sanity — outlaws all.

Barbie's Father Has a Nightmare

Eve Tihanyi

His daughter, now forty,
decides she's had enough,
calls a press conference, announces
that like Xena, she will be
a figure of action, a warrior princess

Put simply, she wants to kick ass,
chide the gods as if they were
delinquent angels, predictable and delicate,
prey to her uncanny prescience

She wants to ditch Ken and teeter
on the highest ledge of pleasure,
dare her newly appointed heart
to commit a fall into erotic turbulence

She wants to indulge in choices of all kinds,
slide into black leather if she feels like it,
spike her hair, have Midge's name
tattooed on her breast, sport
an Athena countenance
as a conversation piece

She wants to dance with turpitude;
relish it

LOST HEROES ARCHIVE
presents
the WONDER GIRLS of JUSTICE
FIVE PHENOMENAL HEROES BROUGHT TOGETHER WITH A COMMON GOAL TO BE THE WORLD'S FIRST ALL-WOMAN FIGHTING FORCE!
THE SPHERE OF JUSTICE
Ms America
Wicked Woman
The Maker
Drama Queen
featuring
Plain Jane
HIDDEN HIGH AND DEEP WITHIN A SECRET LOCATION OF THE ANDES MOUNTAINS THEY MOBILIZE THEIR OPERATIONS FROM THE GREAT SPHERE OF JUSTICE!
Written & Illustrated by Tariq Sami

MS AMERICA
Real Name: Selma Evans
Occupation: Former student, fashion model, and dancer
Age: 43 years old
Identity: Publicly known
First Appearance: *Giant Size American Tales #1* in which Ms America battled and defeated the raging mechanical juggernaut known as Super Capitalistobot
Known Foes: Blithering Boy, The Czech Cheerleader, most recent US Presidents & military generals, Miss America Pageant Commission, NASA
Human Origin / History: In 1988, small-town southerner Selma Evans is crowned Miss America, joining a short list of African American women title-holders. In a scheme of opportunity, The Pageant Commission joins NASA with plans to launch Miss America into space — the television event of the decade.
Birth of a Superhero: Selma's vessel loses power and speeds towards Venus where it is bombarded by mutagenic radiation. The ship is ravaged, but Selma is spared. The combination of alloys in her pageant crown act as a conduit for the radiation, Venusian rays are channeled into her body, and the crown becomes fused to her head. Selma is transformed into a radioactive superbeing and the once-lost-in-space pageant queen returns to earth where she demonstrates a series of dazzling public spectacles. Miss America boldly declares that she will never again be anyone's puppet; she co-opts the title as her superhero name, but changes the moniker to Ms America.
Abilities: Ms America possesses substantial nuclear power which can be focused and projected into powerful blasts of energy. The US Military determines that Ms America's ability increases proportionally in response to it's own nuclear build-up. Her crown acts like an antenna to collect and synthesize empirical data about nuclear growth and supplies her with an appropriate responsive amount of power. Being Earth's mightiest hero, Ms America naturally has the ability to fly.

Ms America
MA
BEAUTY QUEEN
NASA
ASTRONAUT

MAKER

Real Name: Gloria Esteban

Occupation: Former student, factory labourer and temp secretary

Age: 32 years old

Identity: Publicly known

First Appearance: *Amazing Action Stories #119* in which The Maker defeated the evil proprietorial land-grabbing villain known as Ground-Hog

Known Foes: The Action Twins: Weather Girl & UV Boy, Doctor Manipulator, The British Museum, corporate construction companies

History: Gloria Esteban migrates from Mexico City to Los Angeles when she is twenty-one and works as a temp secretary while studying fine art at a community college. There, she meets Elsa Von Lanchester, an engineering student, with whom she develops a relationship. While sculpting clay, Gloria notices a tingling sensation causing her hands to swell and turn to a bright green. Stranger yet, arcs of energy inexplicably spring from her fingertips. Radioactive clay is at the root of the problem! With a trail of crushed keyboards and jammed photocopiers behind her, Gloria's employment prospects rapidly diminish.

Birth of a Superhero: Gloria turns to Elsa who designs two gauntlets are capable of harnessing the new energy. With practice, Gloria learns to focus the power in her hands and takes on the identity of The Maker, a superhero who reconstructs inner city neighbourhoods. On one assignment, she revitalizes an entire Mexican town and simultaneously foils the plans of the evil water tyrant, The Hydrokeeper, which leads to The Maker's membership with the *Wonder Girls of Justice*. Gloria later separates from Elsa to focus on her superhero work and, in a vengeful rage, Elsa takes on the persona of The Manipulator, becoming the WGJ's most formidable foe.

Abilities: The Maker can modify the molecular structure of any organic object. Her energy can melt such objects, but once harnessed by the gauntlets, the Maker is able to regulate the energy at will. She wears the gauntlets on a permanent basis and operates them like prosthetic devices. Once, she repaired the world's smallest motorcycle (measuring a mere 10 centimeters) for the incredible shrinking Mighty Tiny Girl. The young up-and-coming size-shifting superhero later becomes the Maker's girlfriend.

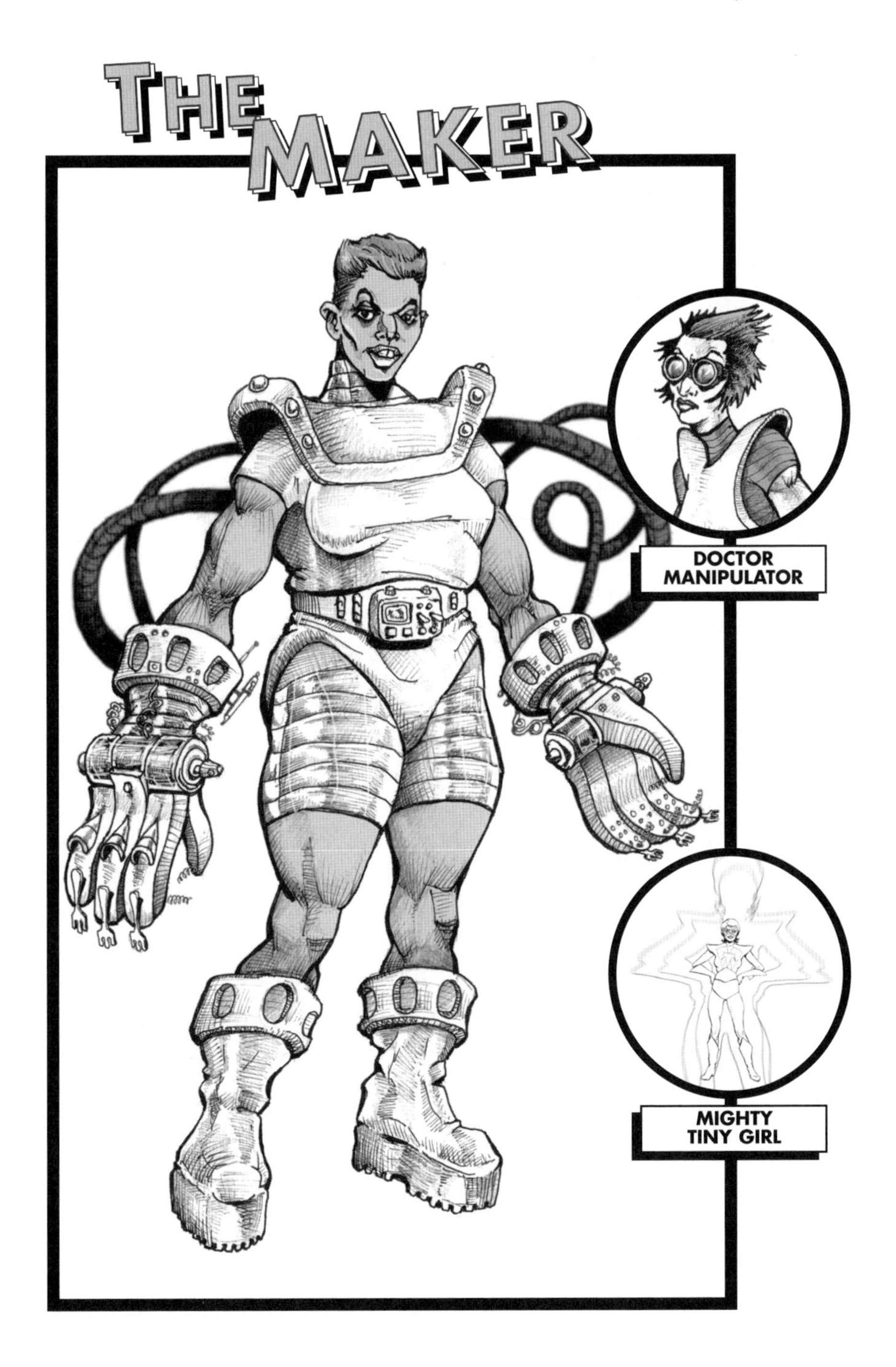
THE MAKER
DOCTOR MANIPULATOR
MIGHTY TINY GIRL

WICKED WOMAN
Real Name: Antonia LeVay
Occupation: High school student
Age: 17 years old as civilian, over 300 years old as Wicked Woman
Identity: Unknown to general public; Antonia Levay and Wicked Woman are not publicly thought to be the same entity
First Appearance: *Tales to Perplex #23* in which Wicked Woman used ancient magic to defeat the criminal scientist, White Collar Warlock
Known Foes: Armadillo Boy, The Apothecrapper, crime duo of Prudent Pete & Pungent Paul, guidance counselors, Max Factor, L'Oreal, Seventeen Magazine, the Olsen Twins
History: Antonia LeVay, a high-school slacker bored with Marilyn Manson, s and Nine Inch Nails, pillages her parents' vinyl collection where she finds a curious-looking Stevie Nicks record. While playing it backwards, metaphysical ethers are siphoned and Antonia is transformed into the once dormant crone spirit, Wicked Woman.
Birth of a Superhero: 300 years earlier in Massachusetts, Abigail Abercrombie Fitch is burned at the stake for suspected witchcraft; fearful of her wicked wraith, townsfolk call her "Wicked Woman." Antonia is Wicked Woman reborn, fighting injustice with an array of magical wiccan powers and divine amulets at her disposal. Employing a derivative Stevie Nicks inflection, Antonia utters words from the famous song *Rhiannon* in reverse sequence, "ssenkrad eht si ehs neht dna, krad eht ni tac a ekil si ehs" (she is like a cat in the dark, and then she is the darkness), and is granted the power of the ancient goddess.
Abilities: Wicked Woman is able to move large objects from great distances, teleport at will, and fly with the aid of her super witch boots. Her good deeds are recognized by Ms America, particularly her defeat of the Apothecrapper's salacious attempts to poison impoverished nations with experimental medicines. She joins the *Wonder Girls of Justice* with one stipulation — she is not a team player and will not be expected to behave as such (This caveat allows her to maintain separate identities.) Wary of future spirit encounters, she now avoids Fleetwood Mac records, avant-garde 70s art rock, occultish folk songs, and any contemporary music which seems lyrically prophetic.

WICKED WOMAN
ANTONIA LeVay

DRAMA QUEEN

Real Name: Tomie Arrigato

Occupation: Stage and screen actor, playwright

Age: 27 years old

Identity: Publicly known

First Appearance: *Incredible Tales of Action #78* in which Drama Queen defeated the evil linguistics abuser known as Dr Wilhelm Shakespearer

Known Foes: Mister Roboto, Whimsical Willie, publishing crime duo of Sappy Scribe & Sketchy Scribbler, The ISBN Assassin, The Hairy Hippie, Cecil B. D'Evil, The Casting Grouch, Hollywood, reality TV, Nicole Kidman, Lucy Liu, grant agents

History: Toronto-based Tomie Arrigato moves to Hollywood in pursuit of film work. She auditions for typical parts, including Korean convenience store owner, Asian massage parlour worker, and broken-English-speaking murder witness. Every audition concludes with comments on her ethnicity, lack of "appropriateness" for the role, above-average height, and ample lower body.

Birth of a Superhero: Tomie's abrasive attitude finally lands her a part in a major film, but the role is that of a derivative evil Dragon Lady antagonist with a brief kung-fu scene and dialogue limited to "Me love you long time G.I.'s, but now you die!" Rather than quit the project, Tomie sabotages the set but is mildly electrocuted in the process. The electricity reacts with the heavy lead-based pancake makeup and she is transformed into the ultimate Drama Queen. Discovering that she has the power to magically control the emotions of others, she finds it pointless to pursue acting, and develops her superhero career. She uncrates an old hippie outfit from a performance in *Hair* — an appropriate visual analogue to her powers — and uses it as her costume. She fights film industry crime for two years before joining the *Wonder Girls of Justice.*

Abilities: Drama Queen's power lies in her capacity to affect the emotions of others. She has little quantifiable power in superhero terms, but her ability to compel humour, sadness, anger, and fear are immeasurable. Drama Queen's trademark: she embarrasses supervillains into surrender by compelling fits of laughter that cause them to wet their pants rather than engage in combat.

TOMIE as the DRAGON LADY

PLAIN JANE

Real Name: Jane Van Ark

Occupation: Homemaker

Age: 36 years old

Identity: Secret, with various aliases

First Appearance: *Astonishing Science Adventures #108* in which Plain Jane orchestrated a massive east coat power blackout to impede unethical business practices of the criminal mastermind known as Dr Hoarder

Known Foes: Delivery Boy, Philips-Head Philanderer, the Money-Changer, Dastardly Dietician, Wal-Mart, Sears, Radio Shack

History: Jane Van Ark, a middle-class homemaker in suburban New Jersey, raises a family which includes two teenagers, a dog, a cat, and two hamsters. Jane spends most of her daytime hours in the pursuit of furthering her knowledge through self-education. She soon discovers a remarkable knack for absorbing and synthesizing large volumes of information without great effort.

Birth of a Superhero: Intrigued by *Wonder Girls of Justice*, Jane hones her skills in science, electronics, accounting, and legal affairs, and offers her services to the group. She is accepted and proves to be a valuable member when she designs the great Sphere of Justice headquarters — a top-secret base for the WGJ that houses famed super-computer Big Momma 1. She adopts a superhero identity as Plain Jane and retrofits her home appliances to conduct advanced espionage operations for the WGJ from her remote location.

Abilities: With remarkable Martha Stewart-like ability (minus the evil undertones), Plain Jane adopts the attire of the suburban soccer-mom, resembling a late 1980s Meg Ryan. Her needs are expertly accounted for: pleated acid wash jeans reserve ample pocket space for hand tools and conceal small electronic devices, shoulder pads holster larger electronic communication devices, and her hairstyle is "volumized" to accommodate video surveillance, camera, and radar devices. Her vision is augmented with intricately designed contact lenses, but she also wears large-frame non-prescription glasses that are, in fact, advanced x-ray specs and video monitors. Her mastery of disguise allows her to assume useful alternate identities such as Jane Barrister, the Lawyer, and Jane Booker, the Accountant.

PLAIN JANE
JANE BARRISTER the LAWYER
JANE BOOKER the ACCOUNTANT

pilot light

Daphne Gottlieb

I've been wrecked by Amelia Earhart. When she's not around, I nuzzle the fuzz on the inside of her leather cap's earflaps, finger the soft folds of her tan aviator's jacket. When she nonchalantly breezes through the room, slings her jacket over her shoulder, matador-like, I thrill to the fact that my fingerprints, the tiniest morsels of my skin, travel with her.

She always knows exactly where she is. I only know by my proximity to her. To Amelia's left. To her right. Five thousand miles away. Beyond my grasp. Right now, she's doing something with a map and a compass at the table, sipping her coffee. Now she's calculating something on its edge. Now she's talking out loud, and I pretend that she's talking to me when she mutters, but I know her sweet nothings are just for the sky, something big, something beautiful, something that makes her free and brave and strong. Something that makes her fly. I'm nothing she even sees, with skin barely the colour of sand, eyes the colour of dirt in the rain. I'm hardly even here.

When I dab plane fuel behind my ears, she sighs the sweetest sound, a dove's coo, breeze through spring branches on a warm night. She swoons slightly, she stirs, she looks up at me. And she grabs her cap and jacket. The air is calling her. That's what she wants. That's where she's going. I know how it feels to want like that, to be pulled, torn apart, incapable of doing nothing but that *thing* that is calling to you. It's how I feel about her.

It's why I've painted myself the idyllic blue of the clearest sky, bought clothes that are nothing but the shiniest silver of the fanciest planes, dyed my hair the serene dark of midnight skies. And I'm still not close enough to what she wants. I'm still not good enough for her. I'm only good when I'm near her. She's the only thing that makes me feel good.

When I hear her propeller stutter overhead, I run outside to watch her soar, feel the sudden cold of her plane's shadow pass over and through me. When I raise my fist up to the sky, stretch my fingers up, it's like I can almost touch her, even when my hand is empty. From that high up, I can almost believe she's smiling down, waving, seeing me see her, loving the reflection, seeing herself soaring over me. She's never more beautiful than when she's completely gone.

~ *The Bollywood Series Presents* ~

Zeera Kapoor: Recollections of a Hindi Filmi Actress

Dalbir Singh

Hello, and thank you for inviting me to this conference on Bollywood screen legends. As you know, my career has spanned a couple of decades and in that time I have worked with many actors. Besides dispelling idle gossip about myself, there isn't much else to say. I would go and do and shoot, and then I would come home and sleep. I never went to the after-parties, I preferred sleep instead. Any chance I could get, in between shots, waiting for director's notes, after a long day of dance upon dance upon dance, I would curl up, close my eyes, seeing darkness, seeing the red flesh of the interior of my eyelid. Sometimes I would picture, dream of my grandmother, my dahdi who passed away on my twenty-sixth birthday. I am forty-six now. Yes, yes, I know.

Anyway, my dahdi was very smart. She knew then, as I didn't, that as each day, each second passed, the offers would become more and more scarce. "What will you do when you're thirty?" she asked. "Dahdi, I'll be dancing on the TV. You will put in the bootlegged video and click the TV on with your remote and like magic I will be there," I would say. One day, I received a call on the set of *Prem Qaidi*. My father, whom I rarely spoke to then, simply said, "Dahdi has died." He waited for an answer. I didn't reply, and so he hung up.

I didn't go home. Instead, I stayed on the set because the director was in a better mood that day, and the lighting assistants, Ashok and Sanjeev, were desperately wanting the shot to be over and done with. So I was standing at the bottom of a hill at the foot of the Himalayan mountains in Chandigarh, which was supposed to be passing for Switzerland, with the lead actor standing beside me. Before "action" was screamed out by the director – he never yelled, he always fucking screamed – I'm so sorry can you bleep that out? Great. Anyway, before the ghastly scream, the lead actor looked at me, straight in the eye, and do you know what he did? He licked his lips. Like I was a tasty dish. Butter chicken, carrot halwa, gulab jamans. A feast for the eyes, something to be devoured.

And so I heard the scream and the machinations of a cameraman on a crane overhead. The actor leaned towards me and pulled me towards the ground. My body roughly fell onto the freshly mowed grass, its burnt smell invading my nostrils, the stench all around me. His body fell onto mine like dead weight. His eyes filled with hunger; mine were filled with the thoughts of my dead dahdi. I was thinking of her corpse as he inched towards me, mouthing the words of "Yeh Mohabbat Heh." The sexual innuendos coming at me through his mouth, his breath. And I smiled, because that is what I was paid thousands of rupees to do. To smile, and breathe the words someone else puts into my mouth.

I urge you as film scholars to examine and analyze that particular song from *Prem Qaidi*. Because, if you look close enough, you will see that I'm not smiling. That I'm masking the look of death so visible in my eyes. That I'm trying to ward off his hunger with every staged rebuttal of a kiss.

You will be able to see the death of my mother's mother on my lips.

Why I Want to Be Pam Grier

Collin Kelley

I want to pull a gun out of my hair
and blow your head off.
I want to wear black leather knee high boots
and plant my ten inch heel up your sorry ass.
I want to flim you and flam you and just say
goddamn you,
while I slit your throat with my knife.
I want to be exploited, overworked
and underpaid, but look damn good doing it,
'cause I'm always getting laid.
I want to be an idol, a nobody,
a *whatever happened to her,*
then put on my Kangol hat, my tight black suit,
look better than I did twenty years ago,
and smoke you one more time good and proper.
I want to cross 110th Street with a bag full of cash,
and one last sweet kiss from the man
who actually gave a damn.
I want to drive away into the morning light,
headed for Spain, hurting like hell,
but with my head up
and the taste of him on my lips.

Annah, Get Your Gun, karen (miranda) augustine

Afua #1, karen (miranda) augustine

Beyond Dis/Credit: Divine Brown, karen (miranda) augustine

Brick House, karen (miranda) augustine

Artist's Statement

Perception is in the details . . .

My artwork circumvents market-mediated ideas regarding womanhood: issues of self-possession, sexual containment, spiritual ecstasy, and girlhood rites of passage, as presented within the West's mainstream cultural media. Although not exclusively, I am particularly interested in subverting cultural assumptions about women of African-Indigenous lineage beyond the restrictions of slavery-imbued reference, as this tends to limit interpretation to colonial history, restricts ways of seeing, and serves to eradicate cultural and historical dignity. I tend to extrapolate elements of ancient Indigenous rituals found in African, South American, and Oceanic cultures — as well as Jungian texts and newspaper headlines — to explore and revision a certain truth about female self-actualization. The photograph, *Afua #1*, embodies this in its affirmation of heritage, women's sensual spirit, and strength.

Annah, Get Your Gun is a response to Paul Gauguin's painting *Aita Tamari Vahina Judith te Parari (Annah the Javanaise)*. The script is flipped on the French painter's unrelenting hunt for the "noble savage," which led him to create a series of debased caricatures — while acquiring scores of child mistresses — from the Southeast Asian islands and Oceania. In Paris in 1893, the forty-five-year-old Gauguin painted his mistress-model, Annah: a thirteen-year-old Javanese girl, who — not quite as demure as he artistically conceived — would later destroy several of his paintings, disappear with the contents of his studio, and soon become a close "companion" to another French artist. (Paradise lost? Rewind: paradise jacked!) In his original painting, I wondered: Who is the sexy monkey sitting demurely, and who are these indigenous girls whom he claimed could be bought for pieces of chocolate?

And here is the common denominator. *Beyond Dis/Credit: Divine Brown (B&W)* repositions hooker Divine Brown's sexual transaction with actor

Hugh Grant, while *Brick House* is a visual audio sample, securing the b-girl's presence – upfront and centre: a tag, reminding the hip-hop generation of its gender problem; a pound, to the lesser known male MCs who care enough to broach it. I consider them both a response to the press, BET and today's talk show frivolity. For all that working-class and Black teenage/women are claimed to be, why is the oppositional truth not the currency?

– *karen (miranda) augustine*

Nothing Sacred

Lori Hahnel

Things are pretty quiet upstairs. Travis and Noella aren't in their bedrooms. "Travis, Noely," I call into the closets. "Come out now." No giggling or whispering. I do a second round of the closets, in case they're huddled in the back. "This isn't funny. Come out now." Then I notice the front door is unlocked. I never leave the doors unlocked. I turn and see that their jackets and boots are gone from the bench by the door.

I look out the front window, then the back. "Travis!" I yell out the back door. "Noely!" I yell out the front, my voice suddenly sounding thin and reedy. My words disappear into the snow. Any footprints there might have been are covered now.

I tried a new hairstyle a few mornings ago. Nobody noticed, but it's exactly the way Carole Lombard wore it in *My Man Godfrey*, bangs parted in the middle. Probably to hide the scar on her head from the car accident. Wonder what it was like to work on that film with William Powell, her ex-husband? It's just a good thing she didn't live to see that awful remake with that awful June Allyson. Can you imagine?

"See you at lunchtime, Travis," I called as he lined up to go in with the other first-graders. I've often thought about the irony of Travis being called Travis. I'm sure his parents didn't name him after Travis Banton, I'm sure they have no idea who Travis Banton was. Maybe he's named after Travis Tritt, though I don't think they're much into country music. Maybe it's a family name, I don't know. Anyway, it's just funny that Travis Banton was one of Lombard's favourite costume designers. What are the chances?

I let Noely play at the playground for a while, but soon she wanted to leave. "Take me to the store, Ginny."

"We can't go to the store every time we drop Travis off at school. Let's go home and watch Rolie Polie Olie."

She shook her head, blonde curls flying. "No. I wanna go to the store. Travis gets to go to school."

So we got into my car and drove over to the store. I was a little ashamed, a little worried that some neighborhood mom, or another nanny, might see us at Mac's at ten after nine every morning, Noely filling her chubby fists with candy. I used to be better at this, I used to care more. Now, I figure a dollar's worth of candy buys me forty minutes or so of quiet. It's not like I'm abusing her or ignoring her. I just don't want to try to reason with a three-year-old. It can't be done. I tried with Travis, and it was an exercise in futility. But I tried, dammit, I worked my ass off at it, and then I realized his parents let him do whatever he wanted at night, and on weekends. So, in spite of all my work and caring, he's turning out to be a little shit anyway. It makes me sad. I feel sorry for him, too. A little guy with an attitude problem like that in first grade is going to have a rough time of it. Now I can't help thinking there's no point in trying to take the high road with Noely. If she wants candy, she's getting it from me, no argument.

I took this job two years ago, when the old nanny quit. The Martins said they wanted someone who'd be around until Noely started Grade One. Sure, I figured, five years. I can do that. And the first year was good. They pay me well, I can't complain about that. Only I wonder sometimes, about the wisdom of it all, the two-income family thing, I mean. Brad's a plastic surgeon. You'd think that'd be enough money for any family, but Shelley's an advertising executive, says she could never leave her job. The kids were good up until the last few months. Now Travis has this attitude, like I was saying. Noely's getting it, too. Personally, I think it's because kids need parents around more than just for a few hours at night and on the weekend. When they're not working overtime, that is. Of course, I'd never say anything to them. I need this job.

Noely and I went home and read a few books, and then she said she wanted to watch Olie in her room. So I had a few minutes to check out my new magazine.

I took the bubble envelope out of my pack, gently slid the magazine out from its plastic sleeve. It's a January 1940 issue of *Photoplay* I picked up on eBay for almost nothing, only ten dollars. It has that great old-magazine smell, brittle yellow pages. Some pages are missing, supposed to have been an article about Dorothy Lamour. Who cares? Lombard's on the cover. It's a great photo: she's wearing a red and ivory silk brocade skirt and sleeveless blouse that bares her midriff, quite daring for the time. Her hair is dark blonde, shoulder length, off the face. The glossy red of her lipstick is the exact glossy red of her garments. Lombard once said she'd made it in a man's world, but knew part of a woman's job was choosing the right shade of lipstick.

Back when Mom got sick, I quit my job at the video store to look after her. Don't get the wrong idea, I'm not the Florence Nightingale type at all. I didn't really want to do it, but there wasn't anyone else. My brother Jeff had left for Toronto long before. We hadn't heard from Dad in years. I still lived at home, so that was that. The people at work were really understanding. The whole time they let me come in and just borrow whatever videos I wanted, no charge. I didn't watch as many as you might think, though. Looking after her was a full-time job, and lots of nights I was too damn tired to watch movies. I maybe only went through five or so a week. She'd make me feel guilty if I went anywhere besides the grocery store or the video store. She didn't trust me.

After she got a spot in the home, it wasn't so bad. I thought I should see about going back to work at least part-time when she died. Right after that, Brad, who was a friend of Jeff's from high school, called and said they were looking for a nanny. Child care was something I'd never thought about before, but I did have three years of looking after Mom under my belt. And they were offering me over twice what the video store paid, and only occasional evenings or weekends. The thing was, we'd racked up some debt while Mom was sick. I couldn't have said no to the money if I'd wanted to.

Travis and Noely are less interested in staying at the playground after school now that the weather's cooling off. It's too bad, because if they don't work some of that steam off, they get owly by the time Shelley gets back home. Maybe if they dressed warmer, it'd be different. But they refuse to put on their winter jackets if there's no snow, and the wind blows right through fleece. What can I do? I can't make them wear their winter jackets. I can't make them do anything. You can't make anybody do anything; I've figured that much out.

The other day I decided to try setting an example by wearing some warm clothes and letting them see how comfortable I looked. So I wore my cape. It's black crushed velvet, from the1930s. I got it on eBay. It looks like the one Lombard wore to Jean Harlow's funeral. She must have been hot in it. It was in June, in Los Angeles. Maybe hers wasn't lined. Anyway, this one is, and it's so warm. I wore it all last winter. It has a smell of sandalwood; they burn incense in a lot of vintage clothing shops to mask the old clothes smell. But I find that old clothes smell intoxicating. When I smell it, I know I'm someplace I want to be. Then again, I dream about finding great vintage stuff in shops. More than once I've dreamt about a black beaded twenties gown with a spray of bugle beads at the neckline. Does that mean I'll find it some day?

I'll never forget the first time I saw a Carole Lombard movie. It was on a date, the one and only date I've ever been on. This guy Mitch that I worked with, he was really cool. He was into old movies, knew all about them, could always suggest the best one when someone came into the store looking for one. We had a lot of fun on shift together. Then he quit, got another job, and I was kind of sorry to see him go. But he came back one afternoon when I was working.

"There's a screwball comedy festival on at the Plaza right now," he said.

"A what festival?"

"Come on, screwball comedy. 1930s stuff, you know. *Bringing Up Baby, It Happened One Night, His Girl Friday.*"

"Oh, yeah. Right."

"So, *Nothing Sacred*'s playing tomorrow night. Do you want to go?"

"Sure."

Mom wanted to know where I was going. Even before the stroke, she was always trying to make me feel bad about going out, even if it was just for a few hours. I was stupid, I didn't think about it that time when she asked me. But I didn't know she was going to make such a big deal about it. When I told her I was going out to a movie with my friend Mitch, I thought she'd kill me.

"You didn't ask my permission."

"I didn't know I had to. I'm nineteen."

"You still live in my house. You're still my daughter. Who is this Mitch?"

"A guy I work with."

She wanted to know what movie we were going to, what we were doing after the movie, what time we'd be back. I thought of asking her if she wanted to come with us, but I could see she wasn't in the mood for kidding around. She rarely was.

The movie was hilarious. We stopped for a beer afterward, and Mitch entertained me with trivia about it. Like how the director, William Wellman, said Lombard was the only woman he'd ever known who could say four-letter words and make it come out poetry. We ended up getting home later than Mom would have liked. She wasn't waiting up for me, but she was still awake, I could tell. I could hear her stirring about, coughing, heard her bed squeak self-righteously a few times. She gave me the cold shoulder for a few days after that. Then I came home from work one day and found her on the kitchen floor.

Travis and Noely and I used to do something fun, maybe go to the park, or the mall, or out for lunch on school professional days. I used to look forward to them; I was glad not to have to go back and forth to school. Then all of a sudden, I don't know if it was their ages or what, but all they wanted to do was fight with each other on days off school. Sometimes, it took me all weekend to recover.

Last time the weather was nasty, too. So I had it planned out. Luckily there's no shortage of audio-visual equipment in the Martin household. We went down to the video store and picked out two movies each: Travis got *Ice Age* and *Lilo and Stitch*, Noely got *Cinderella* and *Beauty and the Beast II*. I got *No Man of Her Own* and *To Be or Not to Be*, Lombard's last film, released after the plane crash. Apparently she didn't even want to go on that War Bonds tour, but Gable felt his wife's career could use some propping up and insisted she go. Yikes.

So we were set. A movie each for the morning, another for the afternoon. The kids both have DVD players in their rooms, and I used the one in the family room. We stopped and had a break for lunch, and I even took them for a walk, though they bitched about the cold the entire time. Then we got another movie rolling after lunch.

I dozed off in the middle of *To Be or Not to Be*, even though it's a funny movie. But I've seen it before. The credits were rolling when I woke and looked out the window at the big, wet, feathery flakes falling. I turned on a few lights, realized that it was almost five, and Shelley would be home any minute. That was when I went upstairs and found Travis and Noely gone.

I leave the doors unlocked in case they come back while I'm out looking for them. Then I flip on my cell and back my car out of the garage. The snow falls faster, thicker. Visibility is poor, the roads are slick. No kids at the playground. Traffic's a little heavier than usual right now, with people coming home. I feel a little twinge of nausea when I think how easy it would be to miss two little kids who've never crossed streets by themselves, and maybe have no idea where they're going. They aren't at the school playground, either.

I try a few stores at the strip mall: the Mac's, the Dairy Queen, the hardware store. No one has seen them. I run back to the car, head spinning, wet ropes of hair stuck to my face. I'm on the verge of tears but trying to keep my mind clear, trying to push down the little voice in my head that is screaming uncontrollably. What can I do next, what can I do? I take a few deep breaths, then I decide to go back to the house to see if they've come back. If they haven't, I'll call 911.

As I pull up, the two of them are crossing the street to the house. Not holding hands, as they've been taught, but spaced about five feet apart. Both of them are holding bags from Mac's, full of candy, I'm sure. Shelley is standing in the doorway, I notice. I wonder how long she's been home.

I jump out of the car and pull them both toward me, and just gulp in air for a few seconds. It seems like I can't get enough, like I was maybe forgetting to breathe for that whole time, maybe twenty minutes altogether, that I didn't know where they were. It seemed like hours. I stand back and now Shelley's got her arms around them both. She's awfully quiet. I guess it must have been pretty strange for her to come home and find the doors unlocked and no one here and all.

"We went to the store, Ginny! Look," Noely tells me, opening her bag and letting me peer in at the Push Pops.

"We took all our allowance. And we didn't want to wake you up," Travis adds helpfully.

"You two go into the house, now," Shelley tells them. She's standing back in the doorway now, across it.

"Can you imagine those two? Going all that way by themselves? I guess I just dozed off for a few minutes, and look what happened."

But Shelley won't answer, she won't even look at me. What does she want? Everything's fine, isn't it?

How to Be a Saint

Beth Steidle

Beneath the weight of chemicals, three stylists toil over their clients. The stylists look like this:

> X: a gay man, aged forty, with a red mohawk. He puts on a nice show like a good circus animal and tells his clients they are beautiful.
>
> Y: an Egyptian woman, approximately aged forty-five, who has had five plastic surgeries to date. She tells all of her clients she is a lesbian trapped inside a heterosexual body, and she puts Hershey kisses beneath her sweater where her nipples should be.
>
> Z: a fifty-year-old hippie who wants to travel to Mexico to buy one hairless dog. She wants to name the dog something like "Rogaine" or "Slick."

I get paid to sit by the phone, waiting for it to ring. I name my desk Switzerland and declare myself neutral, by which I mean: I am not a circus animal but I pretend, I will not pinch your chocolate nipple though I'd like to, and Slick and Rogaine sound like equally good names to me.

X, Y, and Z bring their clients to the black sinks in the back of the salon. They put their heads in the sinks, cover them with water and soap. The soap smells like pineapples, the aura haloes around their heads, and no one smells the chemicals.

Later, each client will come to me, hand me paper slips with the presidents' faces on them. One woman pays forty dollars to have her dead cells trimmed. The next woman pays two hundred and twenty-five dollars to have her dead cells trimmed and covered in red dye. On and on, et cetera, et cetera. When the register goes *ring*!, I place the bills inside its mouth, then look up and say, *Have a great day, you look beautiful.*

I think then it must be sad to be a dead president and still have the weight of the economy on your shoulders, what with the war and all. I think then it must be sad to have to pay to hear, *You're beautiful.*

The salon's decorative theme is Catholic paraphernalia. The bathrooms are like shrines, dimly lit with pink bulbs and virgins behind glass cases. By the front window, St Theresa cradles a bundle of red roses. She is as tall as my leg, a hollow form of resin. My pencil holder is shaped liked the Virgin Mary.

So to recap: each morning I arrive in Switzerland, count the dead presidents, and pull a pen out of the Virgin's head.

When I was a child, my mother used to hand me a big red book labeled, *What Do You Want To Be?* I flipped carefully through it, eyeing each choice. I looked for the box marked "Saint." When I couldn't find it, I checked ballerina, veterinarian, housewife, astronaut, and mother instead.

I flick my pen, I stare at St Theresa, St Theresa with her bundles of roses sent down from heaven. I look out the window. There are no petals in the sky, only bits of snow I pretend are petals.

X comes over to Switzerland. The boundaries, after all, are open, but that doesn't mean I want him there.

What're you doing, my little pet? he asks.

I'm being a receptionist, I say. By which I mean, answer the phone, take cash, smile, say *Have a great day*. Somewhere there is a little mouse running around and around inside a plastic wheel.

X begins by saying, *You know everything I do here is a show, right?*

I know, I say.

When I was a kid, I was put in a mental institution four times, he says.

Really? I say. I think my tone is slightly interested.

When I was five, I was a voluntary mute. All I would say was LIAR and LIES!

Why?

Because that is when I realized all people were assholes. Then, *I don't know why I'm telling you this.*

He walks away, his client is here, he says, *Hello, beautiful.*

When I was a child, I had two voices: the one in my mouth and the one in my head. The voice in my head told me I was going to Hell. I had to a) not take the Lord's name in vain, b) respect my parents, and c) not be a bitch. When I did anything wrong, or anything at all, the voice said, *BITCH SLUT WHORE BITCH SLUT WHORE*. The voice in my mouth said, *No Mom, everything is fine.*

I glance up. St. Theresa has not moved, St. Theresa and her unfailing roses. When I was a child, we had four books of saints, two for men and two for women. I would read their stories and remember their faces, all of them impossibly beautiful with long renaissance features and perfect complexions.

Thanks, have a great day, you look beautiful, I say. Smile.

Thanks, you look beautiful too, the client says.

Have a nice night.

Thanks, you too.

Bye.

Have a nice night.

Thanks, you too. Smile.

Some people hate to leave. I want to remind them of the studies done on the relationship between air-born carcinogens and perm chemicals, but I smile like Switzerland. Smile and nod.

The voice used to tell me that if I ever revealed its existence, it would infect everyone I had ever loved. I had determined I was being possessed by Satan and this was a trial for sainthood. I was quiet and I was good in the face of possession. I waited for the first miracle so I could step towards canonization. Waited and waited. I imagined my face, side by side with St Bernadette.

Hey, Y shouts across the room, above last year's screaming pop songs and the chatter of Z's antiwar rage. *Hey,* she screams, *do you want to see a picture of the fat they took out of my legs?*

I chronicle the week's events in my head:

1. Saw Polaroid of liposuctioned thigh fat.
2. Our house was raided by the FBI under suspicion that the man upstairs is a terrorist.
3. A live grenade was found next door to the salon.
4. Lover's bank account is minus one thousand dollars for some strange, undisclosed reason.
5. Hallucinated that lover turned into a cat.

Last week, I told my lover about the voice in my head. Now my disease is spreading. She says it's all coincidence, but this is hard to believe. I have stopped using the ATM machines and am concerned about how I will deposit my checks. I believe there are video cameras in the bushes lining Mass Avenue. I believe there is a man in Nebraska monitoring my movements, typing down the seconds in the life of a saint.

Z wants her totals, she is done for the day.

What do you think about "Baldy"? she asks.

It sounds like a great name, I say.

When everyone has left, I am alone in the salon, printing out a million sheets of paper with numbers and codes, and the credit card machine is grinding. The lights are out, there is nothing left on except the neon strands of hair wadded on top of the mannequins' heads. The yellow and green and pink strands drift across the idle stations, turning the jars of barbicide to a gaunt blue, the skeletons of combs and brushes cradled inside.

The sky is dark, and the snow is falling thickly. I look at St Theresa, stare hard. Her mouth blurs, then clears, then blurs again. I walk over to her, touch her painted lips. They blur beneath my fingertips. She is speaking to me, the first miracle, and I cannot hear a sound.

Bitter Mary

McKinley M. Hellenes

I)

Tattoo the world across me I
want no fixed address   no chance to
displace me mis place
me   place me at all
this body is my one residence
and it is only half
                    full

I walk this earth in
someone else's skin in whiteface
white body pink nipples soft
in my t-shirt   brown rock
turned to limestone in my sleep
gotta learn to chip it off before it
turns too thick congeals over me like a
little kid who
pulled a face for too long   folks
get to believing it's really you
that face that cunning

disguise

Even my cunt
someone else's   another mouth to feed
with what I don't want inside me
what is all this flower bullshit
my cunt is tooth and bone my cunt is ragged black incisor
I will scrape out my name   every surface I squat over

will be mine   for once territorial pissings my
acrid pictoglyph

II)

Oh hear me thou grandmothers
hear this daughter
I never meant to spring from you
this way they hid you from me,
grandmothers — slapped pasty shellac over you and
none the wiser   no more wisdom
bleeding from your corner
only placenta same florid colour
no matter the shade of the woman
who birthed it out

Grandmother No-Name:
it's what I call you not quite as distinctive
as Grandma Moses but
what can you do they
probably called you something else
anyway

like Alice or
Mary (always Mary
the word for bitter in Hebrew
what do you need of it, Grandma —
though bitter sounds about right)
maybe they called you nothing at all
hey girl hey brownskin hey
whore hey

Couldn't wait
to get yourself into a white
man's pants could you couldn't wait

to get yourself a bellyful
belly-full full at last full
as the moon your only sister
in this land where brown earth and
brown woman
have the same fate

crushed
like rocky soil
in a white man's fist
no blood from a stone equals
no bloodguilt

But oh brown virgin —
how your blood cries from the ground I will
scoop it up may the red earth seep in
may I taste you in my sweat

at last
bitter to the tongue but
belly sweet.

Lilith

JP Hornick

So God created man in his own image, in the image of God created he him; male and female created he them.

– Genesis 1:27

And the LORD God said, It is not good that the man should be alone; I will make him an help meet for him.

And out of the ground the LORD God formed every beast of the field, and every fowl of the air; and brought them unto Adam to see what he would call them: and whatsoever Adam called every living creature, that was the name thereof.

And Adam gave names to all cattle, and to the fowl of the air, and to every beast of the field; but for Adam there was not found an help meet for him.

And the LORD God caused a deep sleep to fall upon Adam and he slept: and he took one of his ribs, and closed up the flesh instead thereof;

And the rib, which the LORD God had taken from man, made he a woman, and brought her unto the man.

And Adam said, This is now bone of my bones, and flesh of my flesh: she shall be called Woman, because she was taken out of Man.

Therefore shall a man leave his father and his mother, and shall cleave unto his wife: and they shall be one flesh.

And they were both naked, the man and his wife, and were not ashamed.

– Genesis 2:18-25

From the beginning, there was a sense of impending doom. In any story that starts off with such a sense of precedent — as hers does — that really doesn't come as a surprise. There is, as well, the question of the edits. She vanished suddenly from the scene, her presence suggested by a doubling of events, a magician's trick during which she vanishes, a shadow cast upon the other woman. Left out of the standard versions of this tale, she is recovered only much later in obscure translations by men obsessed with the question of obedience and troubled by the products of their own nocturnal desires.

She is an archetype — the tale of a diva and the men who love her, but can't quite measure up. She slipped out to the wings, watching through her reflection as they clamoured toward her door. And she had them all at "Hello."

Lilith was art before form, the cusp of beginning, a moment of inspiration. Wild and certain, when she touched something, she became part of it. She loved with abandon and was adored in return. She knew how to wait, and watch. She liked to watch.

She had always known Adam, and she knew from the first that they wouldn't last. He couldn't sit still, couldn't wait, and his nervous energy set her teeth on edge. He always wanted more; wouldn't be satisfied until he had made his mark on the world, he claimed.

"Adam," she said as he paced in front of her, "we have everything we need right here, an eternity to explore. Sit, rest for a minute." She reached out her hand.

When she touched him, he was afraid. Her skin against his opened worlds to him, a void. There was too much there to fill, and no signpost to bring him back. After their first time together, he fled.

He remembered he had opened his eyes and seen her there for the first time. She rolled into him, feral in her want, body sliding against his, and he came. He wasn't ashamed, simply shocked at the strength of his own desire. He hardened again, fell against her, and was lost. They spent days locked together, exploring the possibilities in the other, no guide but instinct. "Bite me," she said, and her flesh filled his mouth. She licked the salt from his chest and sighed. "I want to know you," she whispered. "Lilith," he murmured, closing his eyes, lips pursed against her breast.

His space changed with her in it. There are dogs here, he said, and monkeys. A pair of rhinos wandered by, and his lips moved around their spherical syllables. He slept, dreaming of his sounds. When he woke, stiff, he needed distraction. A place removed from his linguistic battleground.

"You, and I, and them," she murmured, liquid in her gaze. She turned from him.

"What," he asked, "do you want?"

"Now," she replied, moving away. He looked at a pair of giraffes, told her what he saw. For as long as he could remember, he craved order. Rearranged plates at dinner, asked her to fold the napkins to his liking. She stroked the linen lightly between her fingertips, and he felt alone. Naked. He walked away and she stayed there, fixated. A stroke of stone fixed his spine as he strode away, the first layer keeping them apart.

She shrugged when he returned. Standing there, lost and mute, he couldn't remember why he needed to come back. Lilith waited for a moment, then turned to study the delicate architecture of a peony. He lashed out at her curved, indifferent back; he swelled with his rage. "This is all mine," he claimed, and reached past her for the flower. He shook it in her face. "Without me, this is nothing!" She stood gazing at him, silent, stunned, yet unmoved. "Without you," she said, "that is still a peony."

She plucked a petal from the bruised stalk in his fist and moved off deeper into the woods. He wept, and trampled the remains of the world she had been studying so intently. Exhausted, he returned to his cataloguing. "Peony," he whispered.

Lilith lay back on the soft moss, absently stroking herself and the ground, concentrating on texture and scent, listening to the song of a nearby bird. "Sparrow," she thought, as the bird landed on a low branch over her head. She blinked against the sun and stretched. She wanted to find Adam; wanted to touch his skin and feel him next to her. It had been days since they had last spoken.

She found him hunched over a rock, murmuring to himself while gazing at a series of insects pinned in place with sharpened twigs. He jerked at her hand on his shoulder, and smirked with bitter pride at her shock. "Rhetus dysonii, Aglais urticae, Speyeria lathonia, Coleoptera, Euchroea clementi riphaeus," he hissed, pointing at each in turn. He grabbed her shoulder and moved her toward a long rock wall. "Look," he cried, triumphant. She heard anxious grunts and snuffling from the other side. An overpowering stench wafted from the enclosure. "I've only just started, but it's going quite well. Now that they're contained, I can speed up the process." Peering over the fence, she saw several dozen creatures, panicked and confused, huddled throughout the small space.

Adam's eyes narrowed as he looked at her. "Where have you been?" he asked. Lilith met his gaze. "Here," she said. Adam's face crumpled, and he felt himself deflate. "Come back," he pleaded, desperate with desire and angry for wanting her there. "I am," Lilith replied and stroked his chest. "Stay," Adam blurted as she leaned in close.

As Adam slept, Lilith woke and steadily worked on opening a gate in his pen. Adam shifted in his sleep. Finished, Lilith curled around him and he cried out in his dream.

Dawn broke across their forms. Adam bolted upright as he surveyed the cleft Lilith had made. "What have you done?" he roared, pinning her beneath him. "What have you done? This is my life's work – ruined!" He screamed in her face as she gazed evenly up at him. "You'll pay for this," he grunted, realizing his own arousal. "I'll make you. Remember? You were made for me. Mine." As he whispered his power in her ear, Lilith easily rolled him over.

She swelled above him. Grew and shifted shape, a goddess taking form. He didn't recognize her, felt himself shrinking. "No, Adam, never yours. I am mine alone. I am." She rose steadily above him, silhouette against sky, and was gone.

Adam sobbed with rage and pounded his fists against the ground. He thrashed and cursed the sky. For what seemed an eternity, he writhed in that place. Then, he ran to the edges of the land he knew and, from the clay he found there, he sculpted his remembrance of her. Exhausted, he wrapped himself around the effigy and slept.

Lilith returned to him that night. In his dream, she was vapour. She drifted above him, enveloped him entirely, then leaned over and filled the figure next to him with a kiss. "Eve," she whispered, and vanished. Adam called Lilith's name in his sleep, and woke to find himself spent upon the ground. Eve stirred next to him, both gift and curse. When her eyes found his, they fell together, hard.

Lilith became a memory, a haunting demon who plagued his dreams. Immortal, she had stood outside them both before the fall. He would tell his boys about her, but not Eve, and Lilith would torment his sons in the night with their own desire. Eve knew Lilith's name only from Adam's sleeping lips, and wondered who this woman was who had come before her.

Eve watches Adam, follows him quietly. "This is paradise," he tells her, holding her close. Eve tries hard not to ask him why, wants to believe that it's true. They have his walls and his land and his dreams.

She remembers more than he thinks, though, a lingering sensation of a kiss upon waking. Her first recollection. He works so hard, she thinks, and she tries to keep him happy. But she remembers leaving with him, and knows that there was something better.

"Home," Lilith thinks, lying on warm sand in a place where there are no walls. She is sensual and satisfied, every moment of her endless time defined only by the limits of her imagination. She allows glimpses of herself to the sons of Adam, brings them a pleasure they can never satisfy. She shifts before their eyes, and they come. They always come. Looking, their hands grasping or full of offerings, they hope for a moment of her time.

Sometimes, when Adam and the boys are working the fields, Eve slips out for a moment and finds her in the borderlands. They stroll for a moment, hand in hand, and share a waking kiss. There's a language there between them that neither has ever spoken. When Eve returns, she sits, quietly smiling to herself. Adam and the boys avoid her then, tread softly off to other projects.

Lilith returns to tend her garden. "Peony," she whispers.

Biographical Notes

Sandra Alland is a writer, performer, photographer, and small press fanatic. She has also been known to edit, translate, curate, and agitate. Her work has been published and presented in Canada, Mexico, Bermuda, Spain, and the US. Recent favourites include *Shameless, dig, Rampike, This Magazine,* and *My Lump in the Bed: Love Poems for George W. Bush* (Dwarf Puppets on Parade). *Proof of a Tongue,* her first full-length collection of poetry, was recently published by McGilligan Books. *stumblintongues@yahoo.ca*

karen (miranda) augustine is a Toronto-based writer and visual artist. Her essays, poetry, and artwork have been published in a variety of anthologies, feminist, and art publications. She is the former founder and editor-in-chief of *At the Crossroads: A Journal for Women of African Descent* (1992-1997) as well as the former editor of indie art journal *MIX*. Augustine – aka DJ pussykhat – was a producer on CKLN Radio, which embodied the intersection of Black music, the arts, counterculture, and politics. Currently a graduate student at York University, her area of study is on primitivism, gender, and visual representation. *www.morenamedia.com*

Rima Banerji is a Canadian writer currently living in New York City. She is the author of the poetry collection *Night Artillery* (TSAR Publications). She has performed at multiple venues across Canada, the United States, and India. Her work has also appeared in journals like *Trikone* and *Manushi,* as well as the anthologies *Brazen Femme: Queering Femininity, The Very Inside,* and *Bent on Writing*. Presently, she is completing a new manuscript of poems, called *An Atlas of the Body. anurimab@hotmail.com*

Yes, and it's very nearly normal: meet her for after-work drink, kiss hello (hello Warm), the chair beside . . . until that bit about the wedding she's going to, and the guy she's going with. Oh well, at least it's a story. **Darryl Berger** writes humiliations all the time; they appear in places like *Prairie Fire, Queen Street Quarterly, Geist, Signal, Subterrain, Nashwaak Review, Writual, Dark Leisure, Backyard Ashes, Gaspereau Review, Whetstone, Pottersfield Portfolio, lichen literary journal, Wascana Review, The Fiddlehead,* and *The New Quarterly.*

Michelle Boudreau is a Maritime Métis writer, artist, and activist. She spends her time shit-disturbing for First Peoples', anti-racist, and anti-imperialist struggles in Montreal. Her written work has been published primarily in First Peoples' periodicals, such as *Redwire Magazine.*

Sharon Bridgforth is the Lambda Award-winning author of *the bull-jean stories* (RedBone Press), and *love conjure/blues* a performance/novel (RedBone Press). She is an Alpert Award Nominee in the Arts in Theatre; her work has been anthologized and produced widely and has received support from the National Endowment For The Arts Commissioning Program, the National Endowment For The Arts/Theatre Communications Group Playwright in Residence Program; National Performance Network, Rockefeller Foundation Multi-Arts Production Fund Award, and Funding Exchange/The Paul Robeson Fund for Independent Media. *www.sharonbridgforth.com*

Alec Butler is a performer, playwright and film maker. His *MisAdventures of Pussy Boy* series of animated shorts, including "First Love," "Sick," and "First Period" have been screened at film and video festivals internationally. Most recently, Alec's short films were showcased at A Space Art Gallery in Toronto in a show entitled *Transmissions: Get Your Motor Runnin'.* His plays, including *Medusa Rising* (written under the name Audrey Butler) have won numerous awards, including the Governor General's Award for *Black Friday?* in 1991. *Ruf Paradise* is his one trans man show about growing up transgendered on working class Cape Breton Island. Alec performed *Ruf Paradise* at the Rhubarb Festival in Toronto and at STAGES: the National Transgendered Theatre Festival in 2003. *trans-policy@yahoo.ca*

Dani Couture is the managing editor of *The Danforth Review* and a columnist for *WORD: Toronto's Literary Calendar.* Her poetry has been published in a number of Canadian literary journals and anthologies, inlcuding *The Fiddlehead, Taddle Creek Magazine, Canadian Poems for Canadian Kids* (Subway Books), and *I Do / I Don't: Queers on Marriage* (Suspect Thoughts Pres). Her first poetry chapbook, *midnight grocery,* was published in 2004 by believe your own press. She currently lives in Toronto. *www.danicouture.com*

Rose Cullis is a Toronto-based writer/performer. Her play *The Happy Woman,* was produced as part of Toronto's SummerWorks Theatre Festival in 2004. She recently won an award from Fund (Script Development Program) to develop a screenplay of her play *Baal.* Her poetry and short fiction has appeared in *Torquere: Journal of the Canadian Lesbian and Gay Studies Association, The Church Wellesley Review,* and in the anthology *Geeks, Misfits and Outlaws. rosecullis@rogers.com*

Roxanne Dunbar Ortiz is an activist, historian, and writer living in San Francisco. She grew up working-class in rural Oklahoma. Author of 7 books on indigenous peoples, her most recent books are literary memoir: *Red Dirt: Growing Up Okie* (Verso, 1997); *Outlaw Woman: Memoir of the War Years, 1960-1975* (City Lights, 2002); and *Northern: With Sandinistas and Miskitus in the US Contra War* (South End, 2005). Her next book features Belle Starr, the Oklahoma "Bandit Queen." *www.reddirtsite.com*

Lisa Foad is a Toronto-based writer, performer, theory geek, and pop culture junkie whose work has been published in *Exile: The Literary Quarterly Anacoenisis, Geeks, Misfits and Outlaws* (MiGilligan), and workshopped through Nightwood Theatre in association with their annual playwriting development program Groundswell. She is one-third of the queer femme word-based multimedia performance troupe Trash & Ready, and is the author of *All the Right Answers* (Exile Editions, Darkhorse Series).

San Francisco-based poet **Daphne Gottlieb** stitches together the ivory tower and the gutter just using her tongue. She is the editor of *Homewrecker*, an anthology about adultery, and the author of three books of poetry: *Final Girl* (2003), *Why Things Burn* (2001), and *Pelt* (1999). She was the winner of the 2003 Audre Lorde Award for Poetry and a 2001 Firecracker Alternative Book Award. She is the poetry editor for *Other* magazine and *Lodestar Quarterly* and her work frequently appears in journals and anthologies. *www.daphnegottlieb.com*

Linda Dawn Hammond is a freelance writer, photojournalist, and web designer. As a photo-based artist, she has participated in numerous solo and group exhibits and is currently exploring web-based interactive media as a venue for her rantings. A Montrealer in heart and spirit, she now physically resides in Toronto. *www.dawnone.com/exhibit.html*

Lori Hahnel's short fiction, nominated for the 2002 Journey Prize, has appeared in journals including *The Amethyst Review, lichen literary journal, Forum,* and *FreeFall*, where it won honorable mention in its 2003 fiction contest. Her reviews and essays have appeared in numerous magazines including *Books in Canada, Paragraph* and *Canadian Author*. She is currently marketing a novel. *hahnellm@yahoo.com*

McKinley M. Hellenes lives and writes in East Vancouver. Her stories and poems have wreaked havoc in *The Liar, Hot & Bothered 4, Quills, Kiss Machine, Unimagined Canada,* and *Terminus 1525*. Her short story "Brighter Thread" has been shortlisted for the 2005 Journey Prize. She edits for *Quills* magazine. These stories are for her mom, and for Bergie Solberg.

JP Hornick is a Toronto-based writer, teacher, and ex-pat. Her work has also appeared in the anthology *Geeks, Misfits and Outlaws* (2003). Her collaborative video (with Leslie Peters), *Elephant Gerald Wants to Sing*, based on her children's story of the same title, premiered at the 2004 Inside Out Lesbian and Gay Film and Video Festival.

Susan Justin is a multidisciplinary artist. She has been drawing since she could hold a pencil. Her love for art motivated her to study graphic design. After years of airbrushing out nipples on bra ads and such, she is now applying her training and years of professional experience, in the creation of comic zines, films, paintings, and whatever else her pencil spits out. She lives with her imaginary dog in Toronto, Canada. *www.susanjustin.com*

Atlanta native **Collin Kelley**'s first collection of poetry, *Better To Travel,* was nominated for the 2004 Georgia Author of the Year Award, Kate Tufts Discovery Award, and a Lambda Literary Award. He was also nominated for a 2005 Pushcart Prize. Kelley's poetry has appeared in *Terminus, The Pedestal, SubtleTea, Lily, Blaze, Poetry Super Highway, Welter, Offerings, Velvet Mafia,* and many others. He also produced a spoken word compilation, *HalfLife Crisis,* with musician Denton Perry. Kelley hosts the Internet poetry talk show, *The Business of Word*s, for Leisure Talk Radio. *www.collinkelley.com / www.collinkelley.blogspot.com*

Jennifer Linton was born in North Vancouver, BC and currently lives and works in Toronto. In 1992, she completed the co-operative Art & Art History program and was simultaneously awarded a Bachelor of Arts degree from the University of Toronto and a Fine Arts Diploma from Sheridan College in Oakville. Linton has been the recipient of numerous awards and grants, including from the Canada Council for the Arts, the Ontario Arts Council, and the Toronto Arts Council. *www.jenniferlinton.ca*

Michelle Mach is a librarian and writer living in Colorado. "How to Become a Rodeo Queen" was a finalist for a 2004 Derringer Award, given annually by the Short Mystery Fiction Society. *http://fiatslug.com*

Suzy Malik is a visual artist based in Toronto. Her work has appeared in *Xtra!, Capital Xtra!, Xtra! West, Limbo, Trade, Siren,* and *Fireweed*. She's worked with Few'll Ignite Sound, Buddies in Bad Times Theatre, and McGilligan Books. More of her collaborative works with Zoe Whittall can be found in their self-published comic *Self-Serve* and the anthology *Brazen Femme: Queering Femininity* (Arsenal Pulp, 2002). *www.suzymalik.com*

Jessica Melusine is a writer and bon vivant who has obtained two M.A. degrees in 18th Century British Literature, appeared on HBO's *Real Sex* and Playboy TV's *Sexcetera* and modelled for sites such as *Faeriefantasies.com, Thatstrangegirl.com,* and *Ssspread.com*. Her work appears in nonfiction collections such as *Paying for It,* and in anthologies including *Zaftig, Shameless: Women's Intimate Erotica,* and the forthcoming *Glamour Girls: Femme/Femme Erotica*. She has performed at Ladyfest Bay Area, Ladyfest Ohio and Ladyfest East and publishes the zine *Houri for Hire. www.jessicamelusine.com*

Lenelle Moïse creates personal/political texts about the spirits in sexuality, masculinities, being bicultural (Haitian-American), and other intersecting indentity markers. She co-wrote the award-winning *Sexual Dependency,* a feature film about cross-cultural "machismo," and earned her MFA in Playwriting from Smith College in 2004. Equipped with a few hand-made scrolls, three self-published chapbooks, and a strut beyond her twenty-five years, Lenelle performs her solo show, Womb-Words, Thirsting at theatres and universities across the US. *www.lenellemoise.com*

Allison Moore is an Australian freelance writer/motion graphic designer/bad singer. She has written for magazines, theatre, and film.

She has worked in television and theatre, and now enjoys the flexibility of freelancing and travelling. Allison is currently based in London.

Barbara Jane Reyes was born in Manila, Philippines and raised in the San Francisco Bay Area. She received her undergraduate education at UC Berkeley and is currently a MFA candidate at San Francisco State University. Her work has appeared or is forthcoming in *Asian Pacific American Journal, Interlope, Luna, Nocturnes Review, North American Review,* and *Tinfish.* She is the author of *Gravities of Center* (Arkipelago Books Publishing, 2003).

Tariq Sami has been a graphic designer and illustrator since the early 1990s, working primarily with non-profits and arts organizations. He has also worked for many years as a researcher in the area of post-secondary education. Most recently he has been developing and designing promotional/educational material related to justice and legal rights for youth. If Tariq had a super-power, it might be one that allows him to somehow transform into a teenage goth girl (for the wicked fashions alone) and have the license to wear a utility belt (for the tactical gadget advantage). He would probably call himself The Gothmother!

Sara Elise Seinberg writes things and makes photographs. She is working on a feature length screenplay with Silas Howard; the photographs for a correspondence book with Michelle Tea entitled *Joys and Monstrosity,* a film with Samuael Topiary entitled *Landscape with the Fall of Icarus,* and on her own project, a collection of stories about image. She has a handsome dog called Gus, and they live in Brooklyn. *www.saraseinberg.blogspot.com*

Bren Simmers works as a Fire Lookout in the Rocky Mountains. Her work has been published in literary journals across Canada including *The Fiddlehead, Arc, Grain,* and *Contemporary Verse 2.* She is currently seeking a publisher for her poetry manuscript, *Ladylike. beesimmers@yahoo.ca*

Dalbir Singh is a playwright and a recent graduate of the Master's Program in Drama at the University of Guelph. Recent production work included the play *Your Palace in the Sky: The Bombing of Air India Flight #182* for the 2005 Toronto Summerworks Festival. Recent publications have appeared in *Canadian Theatre Review, Critical Perspectives on Canadian Drama and Theatre* and *She Speaks,* Judith Thompson's anthology of monologues for women. *dsingh@uoguelph.ca*

Beth Steidle recently graduated from Emerson College with a degree in Writing, Literature, and Publishing. She is currently working on her first novel, tentatively titled *Animals and Their Eatables. Beth_Steidle@hotmail.com*

Eva Tihanyi teaches English at Niagara College in Welland, Ontario. She is also a freelance book reviewer and amateur photographer. Her most recent poetry collection is *Wresting the Grace of the World* (Black Moss, 2005). She writes, to paraphrase Robert Bresson, for the same reason she takes photographs: to make visible what otherwise might not have been seen. *creative.power@cogeco.ca*

Zoe Whittall is the author of *The Best Ten Minutes of Your Life* (McGilligan, 2001), and the editor of *Geeks, Misfits and Outlaws* (McGilligan, 2003). She performs with the high femme poetry arcade Trash & Ready, and her next book *Bottle Rocket Hearts* is due out soon. *www.trashready.com* or *www.spencersaunders.com/zoe*

About the Editor

Anna Camilleri has been hailed as a "tough, visceral and funny" (*Atlanta Journal Constitution*) "cultural agitator and fab femme" (*Now Magazine*) – "this lady in red has an important message to share" (*Quill and Quire*). She has performed for the last decade in Canada and the US in theatres, festivals, universities, and in houses of ill-repute. Recent work includes the one-woman show *Sounds Siren Red* (Red Dress Productions), performance installation *Poetry Is Not a Luxury* (Mayworks), and the experimental documentary *Red Dress* (CBC Radio 1, Outfront). In Toronto, her hometown, she has also curated performance programs for the Mayworks Festival of Working People in the Arts, Buddies in Bad Times Theatre, and Inside Out, and she has recently begun to exhibit her visual (linocut and mosaic) work.

She is the author of *I Am a Red Dress: Incantations on a Grandmother, a Mother and a Daughter* (Arsenal Pulp Press, 2004), co-author of *Boys Like Her: Transfictions* (Press Gang Publishers, 1998), and co-editor of *Brazen Femme: Queering Femininity* (Arsenal Pulp Press, 2002). Her writing has been alternately described as "brave and necessary" (*Books in Canada*); "provocative and evocative" (*Xtra!*); "genuine and unflinching," and as "speaking eloquently of the need for civil rights for all of us" (*Lambda Book Report*). *annacamilleri.com*

Acknowledgements

A big thank you to the good folks at Arsenal Pulp Press: Brian Lam, Robert Ballantyne, Shyla Seller, Tessa Vanderkop, Janice Beley, Linda Field, and Nicole Marteinsson. I am especially grateful to my publisher Brian Lam for his editorial assistance. Thanks to Blaine Kyllo for feedback and support in the early stages; stalwart Bobby Noble; Suzy Malik for the beautiful cover art; Tristan R. Whiston for his help, feedback, and for listening to the minutiae with enthusiasm; and to the contributors for inspiring me to imagine female icons through all time, and beyond—in the red light of a new dawning.